Vow of
Evil

VERONICA BLACK

ROBERT HALE · LONDON

© Veronica Black 2004
First published in Great Britain 2004

ISBN 0 7090 7690 8

Robert Hale Limited
Clerkenwell House
Clerkenwell Green
London EC1R 0HT

The right of Veronica Black to be identified as
author of this work has been asserted by her
in accordance with the Copyright, Designs and
Patents Act 1988.

2 4 6 8 10 9 7 5 3 1

Typeset in 11½/14 Souvenir
Derek Doyle & Associates, Liverpool.
Printed in Great Britain by
St Edmundsbury Press, Bury St Edmunds, Suffolk.
Bound by Woolnough Bookbinding Limited.

'In every day and age, Sister, evil creeps in. In every town, every village, like some deadly virus that poisons all it touches. The same fight since the beginning of time. Don't imagine for one moment that anyone is immune and don't imagine either that anyone is incapable of fighting it.'

Brother Cuthbert

ONE

'It's an awfully long time since Sister Joan found a dead body,' Sister Gabrielle observed, as they took their places in the parlour.

'Sister!'

Mother Dorothy who was already seated behind the large, flat-topped desk which dominated what was now the prioress's parlour but had once been the silk panelled drawing-room of the Tarquin house raised her sparse brows above the curve of her round spectacles and shook her head slightly.

Sister Gabrielle who, verging on ninety, reserved the mind of a much younger person and spoke it on almost every occasion, spoke it again.

'You can't say that life is bubbling with excitement round here,' she protested. 'I find the occasional murder quite exhilarating myself.'

The prioress heroically held her tongue. Even verging on ninety Sister Gabrielle had become more outspoken than ever. Neither tact nor discretion had ever been her favourite words and, as she approached what must surely be her last decade, she had taken to making the most candid remarks in her still vigorous voice and with a decided glint in her eye that showed she knew exactly what she was about.

'I'll try and find one for you, Sister, the next time I take Lilith for her exercise,' Sister Joan said, amused.

'Thank you, Sister Joan. May we now get down to business?' Mother Dorothy said repressively.

'Sister Hilaria isn't here yet,' Sister Perpetua reminded them. It was not unusual for the novice mistress to be late since on her way over from the postulancy she was liable to wander elsewhere in the grounds led by some inward vision that quite blotted out her original intention.

'Here she is now!' Sister Marie, newly professed and full of beans, announced the fact brightly.

'My apologies, Mother. Do forgive me, Sisters!'

Sister Hilaria inclined her tall thin frame to kiss the shiny wooden floor.

'What delayed you, Sister?' Sister Gabrielle enquired.

'I couldn't find any of the postulants,' Sister Hilaria said, taking her seat. 'Then I remembered that I had none.'

She spoke the words on a dying fall and glanced about her for an instant as if some eager young religious might have crept into a corner or hidden under the desk.

It was sad for her, Sister Joan, her own eyes clouding over with sympathy, thought. Sister Hilaria didn't seem complete without a couple of postulants trailing after her, the more observant among them gently guiding her in the right direction. Alone she was Mother Carey without her chicks.

'One of the reasons why this meeting has been called,' Mother Dorothy said, rapping her pencil on the desk, 'is to discuss the present sad situation. As our bishop has made clear vocations are becoming scarce in every Order. The Daughters of Compassion cannot hope to escape the prevailing secular wind which blows across Christendom. We are a small Order but we have our role to play and the shortage of novices is worrying.'

'Also lonely for Sister Hilaria,' Sister Mary Concepta observed in her gentle voice. 'All alone in the postulancy.'

'Alone?' Sister Joan, who was about to say that when wrapped in her meditations Sister Hilaria was less alone than anyone she knew, caught Mother Dorothy's gimlet glance and refrained.

'As we already know,' Mother Dorothy said, putting the tips

8

of her fingers together, 'Sister Teresa, our excellent lay sister, was called away to care for her ailing father and is unlikely to return for some considerable time and Sister Bernadette was dispatched to the mission fields by the mother house six months ago. Our loss is their gain.'

'And there are no new postulants for this year,' Sister Martha said sadly.

'It occurred to me,' Mother Dorothy said briskly, 'that with two spaces in the main house and the postulancy itself originally a dower house for the Tarquin family, that it would profit us to rent out the latter for a year or two. There are many nice little families who would appreciate a home at a very moderate rent. The building is separated from the main grounds by the old tennis courts so there need be no invasion of privacy from either side.'

'Are we broke then?' Sister Gabrielle demanded.

'Not at all, Sister.' The prioress frowned slightly. 'As you know my godmother died two years ago and left a considerable sum of money and her house in Devon to me, all of course to be shared with the Order. Two families have since rented the Devon property, but the last tenant left for the United States some weeks ago. Doubtless other tenants will come. In the meantime Community Charges and taxes continue to rise and goods become more expensive and there can be no question of neglecting to pay the bills properly.'

'Our Blessed Lord said that,' Sister Hilaria murmured. ' "Render unto Caesar the things that are Caesar's".'

'Caesar didn't charge VAT,' Sister Perpetua said with a grin.

'So!' Mother Dorothy lifted her pencil and tapped the desk with it. 'I shall insert an advertisement for the rental of the postulancy at once. Sister Joan, you had best look it over and make what slight alterations may be necessary for the accommodation of tenants – I shall stress it will be suitable for a family. Sister Hilaria will join us here in the main house.'

'Where?' Sister Perpetua enquired.

'Sister Joan can take Sister Teresa's cell next to Sister

Marie,' Mother Dorothy said, and nodded approvingly as Sister Joan smiled. 'Then Sister Hilaria can take Sister Joan's cell.'

'I would be quite happy near the kitchen,' Sister Hilaria said mildly.

'But it would be convenient for me to be near the stable,' Sister Joan said promptly and sincerely. 'I can take Lilith and Alice out then without disturbing the rest of you.'

'Then that's settled,' Mother Dorothy said. 'These slight changes will be the last I shall undertake as prioress.'

'You're not leaving too?' Sister Katherine sounded panicky as if the fabric of her family was being rent asunder.

'Of course not, Sister. I trust to end my days here,' Mother Dorothy said, 'but surely you haven't forgotten the election is upon us. It is time for you to elect a new prioress. It cannot be myself since the rules of our Order clearly state that no sister can be elected as prioress more than twice in succession. For the next five years another must wear the purple ribbon on her sleeve. The voting slips are here. I would ask each one of you to take a slip, retire to a private place to consider the matter and having placed your cross against the name of your choice place the folded slip in the post box in the main hall. You have until recreation at eight to cast your votes.'

She rose as they rose, intoned the customary, '*Dominus vobiscum*', was answered by a chorus of '*Et cum spiritu tuo*', and watched them file out with the faintest twist of regret on her lips.

'Are we allowed to discuss the election?'

On her way into the hall Sister Joan heard Sister Martha's whisper at her elbow, accompanied by a discreet tug at her wide grey sleeve.

'I don't think so, Sister,' she said.

'I was hoping,' the tiny nun confided, 'to have a word with Luther.'

'Luther!'

Sister Joan paused to stare.

'Luther is often quite profound in his estimations of people,' Sister Martha said, a hint of truculence in her voice.

Luther, being a tall, lumbering fellow, greatly distrusted by the local constabulary for his record of following pretty ladies, had attached himself devotedly to little Sister Martha who was the convent gardener, doing her least bidding with all the alacrity of which his brain was capable and so far not adding to his record of female pursuit. To call his judgement profound however was, in Sister Joan's view, overegging the cake.

She was spared from having to answer however by Sister Gabrielle who stumped past on her stick, proclaiming loudly, 'Right, let's get this over then! Mary Concepta, you'll catch your death if you hang around in a draughty anteroom. The voting ought not to take the rest of the day!'

The sisters collected their neatly typed slips, each one carefully anonymous and went their separate ways, the two elderly nuns to the warm infirmary where they spent their declining years, Sister Perpetua to the dispensary where she kept check on the aches and pains of her fellow religious, Sister Martha into the grounds where Sister Joan hoped she was't going to bump into Luther, the others to the chapel. Mother Dorothy still sat at her desk, visible through the half-open door. What must it be like, Sister Joan wondered, to be about to yield authority after ten years of absolutism?

She herself went through the kitchen into the yard where Lilith poked her head out of her stall and Alice, the half grown and entirely rebellious Alsatian sat on the cobbles, tail wagging in anticipation of a walk or a game.

'Not now, Alice,' Sister Joan said absently. 'There's an election going on.'

She sat on an upturned barrel and frowned at the paper in her hand.

The names were in strict alphabetical order. She considered each one with as much care as possible. General elections were more exciting but whichever political party won its representatives were not actually going to decide how you lived your private life for the next five years.

Eight names to be considered – nine if one counted oneself. Could one vote for oneself? Heaven forbid! Sister Joan wrinkled her small nose at the thought of lording it over the other members of the community and forgoing her rides on Lilith.

Sister David? Small and unnervingly like a rather anxious rabbit terrified of not getting Alice anywhere on time, Sister David held down the jobs of sacristan and librarian with unstated ease and had reached the letter R of the series of books about the saints for children she had been engaged on for some years. No, Sister David deserved the right to stay where she was.

Sister Gabrielle? Nearly ninety, sharp-tongued and sharp-witted but too old and too cranky.

Sister Hilaria? Sister Joan's index finger drew a circle round the name. The novice mistress had just learned she was, in the absence of novices, to be uprooted and despite her genuine air of spiritual bliss she could certainly inspire loyalty.

Sister Katherine who was responsible for the upkeep of the linen and spent much of her time making the delicate lace that increased the convents revenues? No, she hardly opened her mouth except to say 'Amen' and even then she hesitated as if she wasn't sure it was quite the thing to do. Sister Katherine would be entirely out of her depth.

Sister Marie? Not long professed and far too young for the burden of responsibility.

'Good Lord!' Sister Joan said aloud. 'I'll be forty-two in March and I'm regarding a twenty-seven year old as a mere child!'

Sister Martha? Hardly, Sister Joan thought, reaching out an idle hand to pat Alice who had wriggled nearer in expectation of a game. Sister Martha would be a tulip out of season if she was removed from her beloved garden and Luther would be miserable and possibly start following strange women again.

Sister Mary Concepta was clearly out of the running with her weak heart and advanced years. That left only Sister

Perpetua who was well nigh indispensible as the infirmarian. On the other hand, she had plenty of energy and a good head for figures. Certainly she could inspire respect.

Sister Joan rose from her barrel, for once oblivious to Lilith's hopeful whinny and, with Alice at her heels, walked thoughtfully round to the garden and its attendant shrubbery. At its edge, a low wall enclosed the cemetery with its neat white headstones, each bearing the name, date of birth, date of profession and date of death of each grave's occupant. There were always flowers on each grave, an exactly similar bunch or spray laid in the one place where all were equal.

She skirted the wall and went down the crumbling steps across the former tennis court where years before members of the Tarquin family had lobbed serves across a taut and pristine net. The net had almost rotted away and weeds forced their access through the stained and splitting concrete. Like the Tarquin family, she thought, vanished into oblivion.

The postulancy, which had once been the dower house where cranky and ageing relatives could be stored out of sight and trotted out for special occasions, stood at the far side of the court, its exterior whitewashed, its roof and floors repaired and strengthened thanks to Mother Dorothy's legacy.

The door as usual was unlocked. Sister Hilaria had a sublime disregard for security.

'Give her the keys of Heaven,' Sister Gabrielle had remarked tartly, 'and the Devil'd be flocking in to play rock and roll on the harps!'

Sister Joan stepped across to the front door and opened it. A narrow hall with stairs directly ahead separated two lecture-rooms on the left and the postulants' recreation-room, library and tiny kitchen on the right.

The wooden floors were bare of carpets, the white walls innocent of ornament save for a crucifix in the library and shelves in which various devotional books leaned against one another as if exhausted by their own piety. In the recreation-room there were jigsaw puzzles and some board games.

She bypassed the two lecture-rooms with their desks and blackboards and went up the narrow stairs. Here on either side of another narrow corridor were five cells and a bathroom. Stripped beds and empty closets bore witness to the absence of new vocations. What was perfectly clear was that Sister Hilaria could certainly not be abandoned without her flock in this cold place. It was also obvious that once the fireplaces had been unblocked or heaters installed and rugs laid on the floors the place would certainly accommodate a family of modest size.

Going downstairs again, she looked in at the tiny kitchen. Since novice mistress and novices ate their main meals in the big house the kitchen, which was hardly more than a scullery, would have to be enlarged, the false wall between it and the library removed and some up-to-date cooking equipment installed. Perhaps a wood-burning stove in the old chimney space?

She bent down to see how difficult any alteration would be and opened the tiny cupboard under the sink where cleaning fluid and cloths were kept. As she had expected everything was spotless, cloths neatly folded, a couple of bottles of washing-up liquid stacked one behind the other.

Not, she thought with a grin, pulling the bottles out, that much ever got dirty here. A mug of tea or cocoa on a Saturday evening after recreation marked the limits of dissipation. No wonder postulants were so thin on the ground!

Black crayon marred the whiteness of the wall behind the bottles. Frowning, she opened the door wider and stared within the cupboard.

SHIT.

The word stared out at her, black against the white wall, clear even in the dusk of a September evening. SHIT.

For heaven's sake, how long had it been there? Not more than a few days in all likelihood since Sister Hilaria for all her vagueness never stinted on any domestic jobs. On the other hand she habitually left the doors unlocked.

14

But who had written the word, inscribed rather since each letter stood out, sharp, black, thick, ugly? Certainly nobody who had had any legitimate right to be in the postulancy.

She was on her feet again, gushing water from the single tap into a basin, reaching for the scrubbing brush and bottle of cleaning fluid.

No use! The crayon was virtually indelible. The letters smudged at their edges but still stood out sharp and distinct.

There was a small tin of white paint and a clean brush in the tiny shed by the back door. To her relief it was still there and she knelt to whisk whitewash over the small offending section of wall.

'Sister Joan, what are you doing?'

The tall, gaunt figure of Luther had lounged up and was standing over her, half in and half out of the kitchen. As usual, he wore faded, patched jeans and a sweater of indeterminate greys.

'Painting,' Sister Joan said, finishing with a sweep of the brush. 'If you're looking for Sister Martha she's—'

'Helping to choose a new prioress. Aye, she'm told me,' Luther said. 'What will become of Mother Dorothy then?'

'She will be called Sister Dorothy again and take her place with the rest of us. There!'

Satisfied, she stood up and began rinsing the brush under the tap.

'You'm painting in a funny place,' Luther commented.

'Yes, well, there was a reason. Luther, have you seen anyone round here in the last few days?'

'Not sisters you mean?'

'Not sisters. Boys, kids. . . ?'

'No, Sister Joan.' He shook his head emphatically. 'Not seen no person like that. Not allowed.'

'Nobody from the camp?'

A useless and rather insulting question, she chided herself. The local Romanies were generally true bred Rom, not travellers who pitched up for a night, smoked dope and moved out leaving a mess. Not that all travellers were like that, she reminded herself.

Luther, who was didicoy and not full blood Romany, shook his head again.

Vandals from the council estate? But they scrawled their words in huge letters on walls and garage doors. And some of the graffiti they produced was really quite artistic.

'So what did you want?' she enquired aloud.

'Saw you coming in, didn't I? Thought you might need something fetched or carried or done.'

'That was kind of you, Luther. You could put the paint pot and the brush back in the shed for me.'

He obeyed, throwing another puzzled glance at the inside of the cupboard before she closed the door again.

'Sister Hilaria will be moving into the big house very soon,' she said as they started round to the front of the building again. 'The postulancy is to be rented out. I don't suppose any of the—?'

'No, Sister, they'm not and I'm not housedwellers,' he said firmly.

'Then it will be to a family that needs a nice home,' Sister Joan told him.

It occurred to her as they crossed the old tennis court that if it was a question of need Luther was a prime candidate. Nobody, not even Sister Martha was quite sure where he spent his nights. In the summer he almost certainly selected a broad tree branch or stretched himself in a hollow of the moor. In winter he occasionally bedded down in one of the Romany vardos and even more occasionally went into the convent chapel and curled up behind the statue on the side altar.

The chapel itself was always left unlocked for the benefit of any troubled soul who might be passing after dark. The only soul who had availed himself of the privilege and then only on the most freezing of winter midnights was Luther and the only trouble he seemed to have was that God might spot him sneaking himself in and insist he came regularly to church.

16

'So I curls up behind the lady and she keeps God away,' he had explained to a bemused Sister Martha and Sister Joan.

'But that is the Blessed Virgin,' Sister Martha had said.

'Aye, whatever,' Luther had agreed cheerfully. 'She keeps Him off me.'

'Luther, she is His mother,' Sister Martha had begun.

'If God were first how come there's a mother around?' Luther had argued.

Sister Martha had looked helplessly at Sister Joan as both had tacitly agreed to drop theological discussion, and Luther had gone off to check on a couple of fledgings whose parents had unaccountably vanished, his thick fingers softly stroking the downy plumage as he fed the open, cawing mouths bits of worm.

'Autumn's here,' Luther announced, as they climbed the steps.

' "Season of mists and mellow fruitfulness," ' Sister Joan quoted.

'Hay needs to be got in,' Luther said more practically. 'So who be going to live in Sister Hilaria's place?'

'We are going to advertise,' Sister Joan said. 'There will be a few alterations to make to the building. Perhaps you might like to help?'

'I'll ask Sister Martha if she can spare me,' he said.

'Thank you, Luther.'

She lifted her hand and whistled to Alice who left off investigating a rather promising rabbit hole and came reluctantly.

'Season of mists and the rest of it, eh?' Luther said, by way of poetic comment. 'Rattling winds and wet mulch if anyone asked me!'

He shambled off and Alice reluctantly followed Sister Joan round to the stable yard again.

Her voting slip was still in her pocket. She marked it with a cross and put it in the post box, then went through into the kitchen where the supper of soup, cheese on toast and rice pudding was being prepared by Sister Marie who shot the newcomer an apprehensive look.

'You don't have to help, Sister,' she began.

'Because I'm a dreadful cook or because you have everything in hand?' Sister Joan enquired.

'Well, you are a pretty dreadful cook,' Sister Marie said with a chuckle that removed the sting from her frankness, 'but I have everything under control. Anyway it's nearly time for chapel.'

'I wonder if everybody's cast their vote yet,' Sister Joan said.

'Oh, I put mine in the box,' Sister Marie said. 'I voted for— Well, we're not supposed to tell and of course I wouldn't – but you might just be pleasantly surprised, Sister!'

A remark that sent Sister Joan hotfoot into chapel where she spent the next hour on her knees gloomily contemplating the remote possibility that she might end up as prioress.

At supper there was a definite frisson of expectation as they ate their mushroom soup and deliciously browned cheese and the creamy rice pudding into which Sister Marie had slipped a cunning handful of currants.

The recreation-room had once been a huge drawing-room walled with mirrors and alcoves in which tall and stately displays of flowers had displayed themselves against pale panels. Flowers and mirrors had long gone but the pale wood was still there between white-painted alcoves.

Two long tables with chairs round held sewing and knitting and basketwork and another table held a Scrabble board and a chess set.

Mother Dorothy came in last and seated herself in her usual place. It wasn't every night she joined recreation but tonight held the tingle of expected change.

'All the votes are in,' she said, in her usual brisk fashion. 'None spoiled. The result is a pleasing one. Sister Perpetua had two votes, Sister Joan one, and the rest went to Sister David who now becomes Mother David and our new prioress for the next five years. I know you will all help and support her as you have helped and supported me.'

There was an enthusiastic burst of clapping in which Sister Joan joined somewhat bemusedly. Sister David as prioress?

Sister David with her rabbity teeth and anxious, sniffling little nose? Sister David who spent virtually her entire life between the chapel where she regularly cleaned and polished as if the Holy Father himself had intimated he might drop in? Who spent the rest of her time in the library over the chapel where she was working steadily on her *Children's Lives of the Saints*?

'I will take over the duties of librarian and Sister Hilaria will undertake the position of sacristan,' Mother Dorothy – no, Sister Dorothy now! – was saying. 'For the first week or so I will also be acquainting Mother David with the mechanics of running the house – banks and bills and taxes etcetera.'

'I intend to do my best,' Mother David said.

She looked slightly flushed and modestly pleased.

'What of your book, Sis— Mother?' Sister Martha asked.

'I hope to finish that without neglecting any of my new duties,' she was told.

'So, Mother Prioress, what are your first instructions?' Sister Dorothy enquired.

'I think,' said the newly elected prioress, 'that we should continue with recreation as usual.'

There was a general move towards the tables where knitting and sewing waited, save for Sister Katherine who took out the Scrabble board and headed for Sister Mary Concepta.

Sister Marie, reaching for the square of tapestry she had been struggling to complete for months, gave a yelp.

'Sorry! Pricked my thumb,' she said, sucking the injured member with a wry expression.

' "By the pricking of my thumbs—" ' Sister Joan quoted.

' "Something evil this way comes",' Sister Marie said.

They looked at each other for a moment.

TWO

'Do sit down, Sister Joan.'
'Thank you, Mother Prioress.'

Seating herself on the stool placed in front of the large flat-topped desk, Sister Joan had a sudden sense of *déjà vu*. Sister, now Mother David, was, though some ten years younger than her predecessor, just as small and slight. It occurred to her that in the main this particular branch of the Order of Daughters of Compassion didn't attract tall nuns. Sister Perpetua and Sister Hilaria were both tall and Sister Gabrielle had been above middle height before age and rheumatism had bent her, but the rest of them were of barely average height and Sister Martha was positively tiny.

'Sister?' Mother David was looking at her enquiringly.

'I beg your pardon, Mother David!'

Sister Joan hastily abandoned the wool she was gathering and fixed the other with a businesslike gaze.

'I decided to talk to each one of you privately,' Mother David said, 'so that any worries you might have or any questions could be dealt with in confidence. As you probably have guessed Mother – that is to say Sister Dorothy ran this house with quiet efficiency and understanding. I hope I can come near to her standard. Happily our Rule is there to set the standard.'

'Yes, indeed,' Sister Joan murmured.

It was said that one ought to be able to write down the Rule simply by watching the behaviour of a perfect nun. Sister Joan doubted if she would ever come anywhere near that standard.

'And since most of our sisters are happy in their present occupations I see no need for change simply for change's sake,' Mother David was continuing. 'Sister Hilaria will make a wonderful sacristan and Sister Dorothy will enjoy her duties as librarian – as I did myself.'

There was an unconscious wistfulness in her tone. Sister Joan said, 'What of your book on the saints, Mother David? Will you find time to finish that?'

'Oh, I think so,' Mother David said. 'I am writing about St Rose of Lima at present – such a charming little saint, and I have St Scholastica researched – I did consider St Sebastian but small children might be distressed by his martyrdom, don't you think?'

'All those arrows,' said Sister Joan.

'The point is,' Mother David went on, 'that I have received a most encouraging letter from a publisher who is ready to consider the book as soon as it is finished. However he does mention illustrations. . . .'

Her glance was both self-deprecating and hopeful.

'You would like me to supply illustrations?' Sister Joan said.

'Not, of course, as a question of obedience!' Mother David made haste to say. 'If it were a matter of the book's publication benefiting me personally then I should never dream – but any revenue from the series would naturally go to the Order. It would be cutting into your time, I fear, for you are now engaged in helping to prepare the postulancy for its tenants.'

'I would love to illustrate your books,' Sister Joan said.

'Only one colour illustration for each saint and then some line drawings perhaps – something amusing and yet not improper.'

'May I read the manuscript?'

'It's up in the library. The light there is not very good but one of the storerooms has a large skylight. This is very good of you, Sister Joan!'

'Actually it isn't,' Sister Joan said frankly. 'I was trained at art college; I even had thoughts of being – well, famous. I never would have been of course. Talent but no genius. Anyway I shall be very pleased to illustrate your series.'

'Twenty-six of them – very slim volumes,' Mother David said modestly. 'In a couple of years – possibly three – I hope to have finished the entire series.'

'You may have to cheat over X,' Sister Joan said.

'St Francis Xavier!' Mother David said promptly. 'Such a boon to the Jesuits! Thank you again, Sister. *Dominus vobis- cum.'*

'*Et cum spiritu sancto.'* Briefly kneeling she went out with a light heart.

Outside, autumnal sunshine striped the grass. She stood in the hall bathing in the light that came through the windows at each side of the main door.

'You look happy!' Sister Perpetua remarked, coming out of the dispensary with a bottle of linament in her hand.

'Mother David has asked me to illustrate her series of saints' tales for children,' Sister Joan told her.

'As well as helping do up the postulancy? You're going to be busy.'

'Oh, I shall fit Lilith in too!' Sister Joan assured her.

'You're a busy bee!' Sister Perpetua said, vanishing into the infirmary.

Had there been an edge of sarcasm in her voice? Sister Joan opened the front door and went round to the back, some of the pleasure forsaking the day. She enjoyed activity, always had done, did that mean that one side of her religious life was lacking in some way?

'We are,' her original novice mistress had told her, 'a semi- cloistered Order. We leave the convent premises only on necessary business. We work at what we can do best and earn our bread, but our main business is the glorification of God, and that is best achieved in contemplation.'

Shutting out the world had never been one of her strong points. She shook her head slightly and went across the lawn and towards the long bush-lined walk that connected with the

23

shrubbery and led to the old tennis courts.

To her surprise as she approached the postulancy, the front door opened and a tall, tonsured figure with a halo of curly red hair about a face made for smiling, emerged.

'Brother Cuthbert! I didn't expect to find you here,' she said in surprise, going to meet him.

Brother Cuthbert had received permission from his own prior to live alone in hermit-like fashion, a permission given, she shrewdly suspected, because Brother Cuthbert was the equivalent of a sorcerer's apprentice in any community, having a heart of gold and no practical skills whatsoever.

'I thought I'd just wander over and see if there was any way I might help out, Sister Joan. Not that Mother Prioress asked me but one ought to show willing, don't you think?' he returned cordially. 'If the postulancy is to be rented out one might lend a hand with a bit of do-it-yourself, don't you think?'

'Yes, indeed,' Sister Joan said, smothering alarm. 'However very little needs to be done and Mother David has, I believe, already contacted a couple of local builders. But how kind of you to offer!'

'Pure self-indulgence,' he confessed. 'I rather fancied the idea of taking up carpentry once. Nice to think of following in the footsteps of dear old St Joseph – but the idea didn't bear fruit. Are you here to conduct some planning for the tenants?'

'When they arrive. Mother David stipulated a family,' Sister Joan said.

'A nice little family with a couple of children. I do hope so. Children always brighten the world, don't they? Where's Alice today?'

'I don't know – oh yes I do! I'm due to take her to the vet's for her injection so, as usual, she's hiding.'

'I haven't seen her anywhere around,' Brother Cuthbert said. 'She may have taken a short walk and be back at the convent waiting for you now.'

'Somehow I doubt it,' Sister Joan said.

'Well, I must get on. Praying to do!' He gave her a companionable grin. 'If you're driving into town later do stop by for a cup of tea.'

'I will indeed,' she assured him.

Brother Cuthbert made his home in a small building on the moor that had formerly been used as the village school. When regulations insisted local children took a special bus to the spanking new comprehensive school on the outskirts of town, the building had remained vacant until the young monk had landed there.

Now she waved him off cheerfully and went into the postulancy. There really was comparatively little to do here, she thought. The tiny kitchen could be opened up to make a larger kitchen-diner and a washing-machine and refrigerator installed and some carpeting provided. Some nice bright curtains too.

Under the sink, the whitewash covered the offending word. The unpleasant thought that other words might have been inscribed in other places, under the beds for example, sent her upstairs to get down on her hands and knees for a close scrutiny. There was nothing.

Downstairs again, she went into the library. Sister Hilaria's own things had already been packed and carried to the main house, but the books still leaned together on the shelves. They could be boxed up and put in the main library above the chapel since she doubted if *The Confessions of Saint Thomas Aquinas* or *The Little Way of St Thérèse of Lisieux* would appeal to any tenants.

She took up the latter and opened it at random. A page covered with heavy black scribble met her eyes. Not a thick crayon this time but ink, smudged and smeared over the page and, when she turned the pages, over the remaining ones. Hastily she rummaged through the remaining volumes, finding the same meaningless, spiteful defacement over all but a couple.

Vandalism? If so it was a curious variety. The books were still in order, their spines undamaged, only the printed words within almost obliterated. Someone, she thought uneasily, had what amounted to a personal grudge.

The books would have to be dumped. She would make some excuse to Mother David about their being mildewed or something. No use in upsetting the new prioress unnecessarily.

She found a large paper bag in the little shed and stuffed the dozen or so volumes into it. She would put them in the three large refuse bins that were emptied, courtesy of the local council, every couple of weeks.

The bag bulging in her grasp she began the walk back to the main house, pausing now and then to shift the weight and call hopefully for Alice.

'Ah, there you are, Sister!' Sister Marie greeted her cheerfully as she entered the kitchen.

'Have you seen Alice?' Sister Joan enquired.

Sister Marie shook her head.

'Isn't it the day for her jab?' she asked.

'Yes, and there's no sign of her.'

'We do need some stuff from town,' Sister Marie said.

'I can take the van in and keep an eye open for Alice at the same time,' Sister Joan said. 'Are you doing the cooking this week then?'

'I'm going to be doing the cooking this week and every week,' Sister Marie said on a joyous note. 'Mother David has decreed that taking turns simply isn't practical so she's given me the job.'

'Bully for Mother David!' Joy almost unconfined sang in her voice.

Though epicurean cuisine was not recommended in the Order she had loathed the whole business of preparing food as much as her fellows had silently gritted their teeth before eating the results.

Breakfast, taken standing up after private devotions and Mass, was a piece of fruit, a slice of dry bread and a mug of coffee. Simple enough! Sister Joan, when her turn came, either found she had left the bread to develop hard edges or forgotten to put coffee in the pot.

Lunch was invariably a salad sandwich, soup, fruit and a cup of tea. Simple in summer but in winter almost impossible to ring the changes as the supply of lettuces, spring onions and tomatoes dwindled and even soup could burn if you turned your back on it for a moment.

As for supper – Sister Joan mentally blanked out memories of potatoes having to be scraped from the bottom of the pan, fish leathery on the surface and raw within, and milk pudding to which she had absent-mindedly added black pepper instead of nutmeg.

'Mother David did think of giving you the job,' Sister Marie said with a teasing glint in her eye, 'but she decided after much thought against the idea.'

'Give me the list,' Sister Joan said, suppressing laughter.

'If Alice turns up I'll keep her here,' Sister Marie said.

Sister Joan took the list, raising her eyebrows at avocados and went through to where the van, used ostensibly by any sister bound for town on some necessary errand but actually seldom driven except by Sister Joan, stood.

She enjoyed driving though Sister Gabrielle had hinted it was only one degree better than her cooking – and how would she know when she hadn't left the enclosure for years? Getting in, adjusting the seat, she cast a satisfied glance towards the bins where the vandalized books were now buried under several layers of old newspapers.

But who had done it? Who had left the ugly little word on the wall under the sink? Not the usual kind of yobbo surely? Not a window was cracked, not a single bit of wood scratched. Granted one could approach the back of the postulancy from the housing estate that disfigured the slopes of the moor, but why would anybody bother?

Her thoughts were tending unwillingly closer to home as she drove along the winding track that turned itself into a road as the moor dipped down into the town.

This was the old town, largely unspoilt apart from a bingo

hall and an amusement arcade. Some of its streets were still cobbled and little had been done to change the outward appearance of the fishermen's cottages that clustered along the ancient quay. The antique shops still had their bulging windows in which ships in bottles, Cornish piskies and framed seascapes jostled with beautiful old silver and copper jewellery.

She braked abruptly as a familiar figure hailed her with a wave.

'Detective Inspector Mill! How nice to see you!'

Sticking her head out of the window she gave him his full, recently promoted, status with pleasure.

'You don't happen to have mislaid a dog by any chance?' he asked.

'You've found Alice? Where? Nobody's seen a sign of her since last night.'

'A young fellow brought her along to the station about an hour ago. Said he'd found her tied up on the quay. Covered in mud and her paw was hurt – don't get in a flap. I took her along to the vet's myself. It's a sprain. Anyway she was due for her usual injection it seems so he's keeping her in for a couple of days.'

'But is she all right?' Sister Joan demanded.

'Enjoying being fussed over when I left,' he said. 'I'll pick her up myself and bring her over when the vet releases her. Have you time for a quick cup of tea?'

'I've the shopping to do – yes, a quick cup then.'

'And don't chip the wall,' he admonished with a grin as she sat back behind the wheel and started to swing left into the station yard.

'I haven't broken a single law all morning!' she retorted, making a neat turn and braking gently.

He held the door open for her to pass in, to be greeted by Sergeant Petrie, also recently promoted and wearing his stripes like a veteran.

'Sister Joan, it's months since we've seen you! How are the other sisters?'

'All fairly well, Sergeant Petrie,' she returned brightly. 'Oh, and Sister David has just been elected as prioress.'

'The little one with specs?'

'She's Mother David now. Sister Dorothy is our new librarian.'

'Give them my best, Sister. I'll rustle up some tea, shall I?'

'Three cups,' Detective Inspector Mill said.

'Right away, sir!'

In the office, Sister Joan was motioned to a chair and looked round. Since her last visit nothing had changed save the calendar on the wall. The main desk held neatly clipped documents and a newspaper folded in half. No sign of any personal clutter, no photographs of family. Alan Mill had a wife called Samantha and two sons both in their early teens and away at boarding-school. She had never laid eyes on any of them, but she was aware that the marriage itself had always been rocky.

A young female officer, slender and blonde in her uniform, long legs encased in tailored trousers brought in the tea. Sister Joan, whose own legs, under the midcalf length skirt of her light-grey habit, were charming, found herself hoping uncharitably that the hair was dyed.

Sergeant Petrie came in and seated himself.

'Not good to hear about Alice,' he said.

'No indeed, but she is going to be all right?'

'Right as rain,' he assured her. 'What I'd like to know is who tied her up on the quay? The inspector here says she was tied to one of those big iron rings where they make the boats fast.'

'Even here there's a crime rate,' Inspector Mill said.

'Vandalism?' Sister Joan sipped her tea.

'Lot of incomers flooding the town,' said Sergeant Petrie.

'Six Algerians and a family of Chinese who wouldn't say boo to a goose,' Inspector Mill scorned. 'However, I admit there's a certain – unrest in the air – can't define it exactly. In fact it's only been around for a couple of weeks – nothing definite. Just – a feeling.'

'More vandalism than usual?'

'Not really.' He sighed irritably. 'Oh, slogans on walls, a bin tipped over – now the kids are back at school there's actually been rather less of it than usual. Benefit fraud of course. That goes on everywhere. An old dear down Fetter Lane reported she met the Devil the other night.'

'The Devil!'

'Slightly senile,' Sergeant Petrie said. 'Trotted in to report that she met him in the old churchyard. She likes to wander around there, tidies up a bit and waters the flowers. Strictly unofficial.'

'Do we know her?' Sister Joan asked.

'Mrs . . . Pearson. Aye, that's the name. Nothing in the story. She was toddling round after dark so likely her imagination started playing tricks.'

'So nothing to account for the feeling?'

'Not a thing,' Inspector Mill said. 'By the way I see that the postulancy is going to be rented out. No novices?'

'Not one,' Sister Joan said glumly. 'There's a sad shortage of vocations all through the Church. No, rather than having poor Sister Hilaria rattling round alone she has moved into the main house as sacristan and Mother David – well, to be strictly accurate Sister Dorothy just before the election, decided to advertise for a tenant or tenants – preferably a small family. We're having a few alterations made.'

'Not with Brother Cuthbert's help?' Sergeant Petrie put on an expression of mock alarm.

'Some local builders are coming to do some bits and pieces. We're hoping for a nice little family. Father Malone might know of someone suitable if the advertisement doesn't produce a result.'

No point, she thought as she rose, telling either of them about the vandalism in the postulancy. In future she'd make a point of reminding whoever went there to lock up securely.

'Give our congratulations to Sister David,' Inspector Mill said, as Sergeant Petrie opened the door.

'Mother David now and I certainly will,' Sister Joan said.

'And drive carefully.'

'I already told you that I hadn't broken a single—'

'Far be it from me to argue with a professed nun,' he said, dark eyes crinkling at the corners, 'but when I saw you your seatbelt was nowhere near you.'

'Oops!' She met his smile with a wry grin of her own and went out to the van, past the blonde officer who was typing as busily as if there was an outbreak of serious crime in this part of Cornwall.

The blonde hair, Sister Joan thought as she climbed up into van, was quite definitely not dyed.

The essential shopping done and stowed in the van, she glanced at the little fob watch pinned to the belt of her habit.

Time for a quick walk to the quay to see where poor Alice had been tied. She dismissed the idea of calling in at the vet's. Alice would only get upset to see her friend start for home without her.

The question of Alice nagged at her as she walked down one of the narrow alleys that gave on to the old quayside.

Here, once, in the days Daphne du Maurier had immortalized, the contraband goods from France had been unloaded and then carried by pony or on the humped banks of hay wagons across the moors to be sold along the borders or left at the doors of certain authorities who turned a blind eye to the smuggling. Today, the river which ran clear and sparkling still down from the heights of the moors, was sluggish and the fish were scarce. Small boats that had formerly braved wind and storm now took visitors for trips across the bay or were used on outward-bound courses.

But something of the old atmosphere still lingered and a few diehards still went out to set their lobster pots, or fished upriver for the still plentiful salmon.

A short length of rope that had obviously been cut with a knife still coiled around the base of one of the iron rings. Stooping to it she discerned golden brown hairs caught in its fibres.

Who on earth had tied up the injured Alice here and then left her? Come to that, how had Alice left the enclosure in the first place?

As official guard dog, though anything less like one would be hard to find, Alice slept in a basket under the lee of the stable roof but was free to roam at will. Certainly she could have trotted through the unlocked front gates or wriggled through some gap in the shrubbery but she had never shown any signs of straying before.

If someone had enticed her away she might possibly have gone. With a stranger? Recalling her dog's universal benevolence to anyone on two legs Sister Joan thought it likely that not much enticement would be needed.

She stood up, looked round and began the walk back towards the main street.

The alley a few yards distant from the one into which she was turning caught her eye. A neat wall sign informed her that the particular alley was Fetter Lane.

There was still almost an hour before lunch. Sister Joan changed direction and headed up the alley, past back gates swollen with damp and bins overflowing with rubbish.

'And in which house,' she mused aloud, 'does Mrs Pearson live?'

As if in answer to her query, a large cat sprang down from the top of the wall, missed her shoulder by inches and gave an indignant yowl.

'Malkin! Inside at once!'

One of the doors was wrenched open and a small, elderly woman came out, almost colliding with Sister Joan.

'You wouldn't be Mrs Pearson by any chance?' the latter said.

'Did Father Malone send you?'

The other, who must have been pretty once and still retained a kind of faded charm in her face, smiled at her.

'Not exactly,' Sister Joan said cautiously. 'Are you a parishioner of his?'

32

'Officially. Unofficially I'm a bit lax about going to church,' the other said. 'You're from the convent up on the moors.'

'Sister Joan. I wonder if I might have a word?'

'If it's about collecting—?'

'Nothing like that. I wondered if you heard a dog whining last night.'

Mrs Pearson, pulling a brightly patterned if somewhat shapeless knitted coat about herself, shook her head.

'What time would that've been?' she enquired.

'I'm not sure. During the night.'

'I sleep very sound and my bedroom's at the front of the house,' Mrs Pearson said. 'It was windy too last night.'

'The convent dog was found tied up on the quay this morning,' Sister Joan said.

'Oh, poor thing! Not hurt?'

'A sprained paw. She's in the vet's now. I asked you because – I understand you do occasionally—'

She paused awkwardly wondering how to frame the question.

'You've seen him too?' Mrs Pearson took a step forward, eagerness in her eyes.

'Inspector Mill mentioned—'

'That I'd seen the Devil. Not that he took me seriously. Batty old dear is what the police think!'

'In the cemetery? After dark?'

'I was setting some of the vases to rights – a rising wind could have some of them over if they aren't wedged right. It took longer than I expected but there's no danger in a churchyard – only memories and a sigh or two. Leastways that was what I believed.'

'What exactly did you see?' Sister Joan asked.

Mrs Pearson pushed her door open wider and stood aside.

'Come in,' she said, 'and you shall hear about it.'

THREE

The yard was cobbled and swept clean. Sister Joan, who had been expecting disorder, reminded herself not to make snap judgements as she followed Mrs Pearson through a tiled kitchen lined with jars, pots of herbs and willow pattern crockery into a larger room which obviously doubled as both dining- and sitting-room.

It was a room that had once been smartly decorated though the two plainly painted walls and the two with Regency stripes betrayed a fashion of the sixties. Photographs hanging on the plain walls were obviously family ones. She glimpsed a younger Mrs Pearson in a printed cotton dress with her arm linked to a taller figure in jeans and open-necked shirt. There was a wedding group further along with the same couple dressed more formally, she holding a large bouquet of flowers rather like a shield.

In the corner, a television set quarrelled with the Victorian coffee table and a long sofa against the side wall hid a blocked up fireplace. Opposite, bookshelves held a couple of rows of books, a mixture of paperback and hardback. Romantic novels jostled with Agatha Christies and Dennis Wheatleys.

'Have a cup of tea, Sister?' Mrs Pearson was already getting out an extra cup and saucer from a glass-fronted cupboard under the bookshelves.

That made two illicit cups of tea, Sister Joan calculated, which meant she would have to confine herself to water for the rest of the day, or accuse herself of greed at the general confession.

'Thank you,' she said meekly.

'Makes a nice change having a spot of company,' Mrs Pearson said, skipping briefly into the kitchen and returning with a teapot. 'I don't mix much with the neighbours – oh, they're very nice but they have their own lives to lead, don't they?'

'Your family. . . ?' Sister Joan ventured.

'Oh, I'm the last of the line,' she said brightly. 'Help yourself to milk and sugar, dear. No, I was originally a Stanhope – not one of the aristocratic Stanhopes of course, though my parents both came from good families. The only children of only children. Now the Pearsons were quite a large clan at one time, but whenever there was a war the men went off to fight and generally didn't come back so there were several widows.'

'Your husband?'

'Oh no, dear! I made my Jim promise when we first got engaged that he wouldn't go running off to fight the first chance he got! And he never did – though it was a near thing when Russia invaded Czechoslovakia! No, Jim stayed here, safe at home. Died ten years ago, dear. Heart.'

'I'm very sorry.' Sister Joan sipped her tea.

'Oh, he wasn't a well man for several months.'

'So that's why you go to the cemetery?'

'Oh no!' Mrs Pearson shook her head. 'My Jim was cremated. Always was an ambition of his. He's over in the Garden of Remembrance – at least his ashes are. No, I go to the churchyard to do a bit of tidying up from time to time. The sexton's getting on a mite in years and someone has to keep an eye on things.'

'Because of vandals – yobs?'

'Not really. Not round here.' The older woman shook her neatly permed head of grey hair.

'But you did see the – Devil?'

Suddenly it seemed the most ridiculous question to ask.

'I did.' Mrs Pearson spoke quietly and firmly, trouble in her face. 'The police did nothing. To be fair there was very little they could do. No evidence you see.'

'What exactly did you see?'

'As I said, I was wedging some of the vases with stones. Really it's asking for trouble to put glass vases on graves. Anyway the wind was getting up a bit, blowing quite strongly. It was getting quite dark but there was a bit of a moon. It kept swimming in and out of the clouds. I was on my knees, wedging a vase and I looked up just as the moon appeared again. And he was there.'

'The Devil?'

'A devil,' Mrs Pearson said. 'Reckon I wouldn't be here talking to you if the Lord of Hell himself had turned up! But it was a devil. Black in the moonlight but with the horns glinting silver and the eyes silver too. Capering from side to side and a strange tune playing somewhere. And then the moon went in again and there was only the dark.'

'Someone practising for trick or treat?'

'Oh no, Sister!' Mrs Pearson leaned forward, hands on her knees. 'It was the smell you see.'

'Smell?'

'The smell of evil,' Mrs Pearson said. 'Evil has a smell, you know – sickly sweet and rotting, but acrid too. It was the smell.'

'When was this?' Sister Joan enquired.

'A couple of nights ago. Late evening actually. Around eight or eight-thirty.'

'What did you do?'

'I came home,' Mrs Pearson said simply. 'I was saying the Lord's Prayer under my breath all the way. The words kept getting jumbled up I was in such a state!'

'But why report it to the police? Surely they couldn't have gone out and arrested—'

'I kept trying to tell myself that it wasn't so,' Mrs Pearson said. Her fingers plucked at the sleeves of her regrettable knitted garment.

'So it might've been someone playing a nasty joke?'

'I hoped someone else might've reported it,' Mrs Pearson said simply. 'Nobody had. Oh, the police were very kind, took my statement – but it was obvious they thought I was a bit touched in the head.'

She grimaced slightly as if the possibility hurt her.

'I'd better be going!' Seeing the small clock on the bookshelves Sister Joan rose hastily.

'You do believe me, Sister?' Mrs Pearson had also risen, pleading in her face.

'I believe you saw what you thought was a devil,' Sister Joan said cautiously. 'Whether it was or not, nobody has the right to go capering around graveyards after dark frightening people. If I were you I'd confine my cemetery visits to daylight hours. Look, I really must go! I'm going to be late for lunch at the convent.'

'Well, it was kind of you to come and see me,' Mrs Pearson said in a defeated tone.

'May I come again some time?' There really was no need, she thought privately, but the old lady seemed lonely. Which raised the possibility she had seen nothing at all and merely craved a bit of company. No, her account had been too brief, too logical for that.

Passing the bookshelves she glanced at a couple of the titles and felt belief shaking.

Psychic Self-defence. Phantasms of the Living. Astral Projection. Mixed up with *The Devil Rides Out* and various thrillers and romances. Somewhat suspect reading for a woman living alone and partial to messing about in cemeteries!

'Any time, Sister,' Mrs Pearson was saying. 'No, Malkin, you stay right here! I hope the dog didn't take too much hurt.'

'I'm sure she didn't,' Sister Joan said.

A moment later she was belting up the alley towards the

van. She was going to be late and she hadn't the smallest excuse for it.

'Sister Joan!'

She had slowed down momentarily by the church when a cassocked figure bumbled out of the gate, one hand raised in either salute or warning.

'Glory be to God but I thought I'd missed you!' He panted up to the side of the van as she braked sharply.

'I'm awfully late for lunch, Father Malone,' she began.

'Have a bite with me. I'll phone the convent.'

'I can't. Lunch is in the van – at least some of it is. Sister Marie is the new cook.'

'Come in for just a moment then. I've a small problem.'

Defeated, she parked the van at the kerb and followed him up the side path to the presbytery.

'It's Sister Jerome's day off but she left sausage rolls,' he tempted, as he ushered her into the study.

'We're vegetarian as you well know, Father, so get thee behind me!' she retorted with a grin.

'Aye, if it were that simple!'

His jollity suddenly dwindling, he indicated a chair and moved to the table to pour out tea.

'No, really, Father – oh, thank you.' I will be awash with the stuff before the end of the day, she thought gloomily.

'When you've heard me out,' he said, seating himself in an adjacent chair, 'it'll be the brandy you're needing.'

'What's happened?' She leaned forward, conscious suddenly that he looked unusually pale.

'You know after I've been up to the convent to offer Mass for all of you I come down and offer it for the general parishioners. I've a dispensation to do that when Father Stephen's away.'

'He's still on holiday?'

She wasn't altogether sorry that Father Stephen was still away. There was something about the sleek, mellow-toned young priest that grated on her. No doubt he was an estimable

39

curate, but to her mind his eyes were already fixed far too intently on a future bishopric.

'He returns in a couple of weeks,' Father Malone said. 'It's by way of being a working holiday for him. He's writing a paper on church murals during the sixteenth century.'

And that would be absolutely riveting reading for the people on the local council estate or the Romanies in their vardos, she thought cynically.

Aloud she said, 'So what's the problem, Father?'

'Finish your tea and I'll show you,' Father Malone said, gulping his own and rising again. 'I have said nothing to Sister Jerome. Happily that particular cupboard is kept locked so she seldom tidies it.'

He was leading the way through the door, down the short passage and through the door leading into the sacristy.

'The cupboard here,' he said in the same hurried manner, 'holds baptismal certificates dating back to the eighteenth century. Of course the parishioners of that day will have been given copies, but the originals are still held here – many most beautifully decorated and, of course, in copperplate script. I would not be showing this to anyone else, Sister, but you have some experience of the world. Your fellow religious would be unable to bear the shock, so they would!'

The carefully preserved, yellowing pieces of vellum looked at first glance undamaged. Only when she held them to the light could she see the nastily obscene little drawings that disfigured almost every capital letter.

'If this were to reach the ears of Rome!' Father Malone said, on a dying fall.

'Has Rome asked for them?' she enquired.

'Thanks be to God, no, but with Rome one never knows,' Father Malone said. 'It might just enter someone's head that a small town in Cornwall in the eighteenth century was worth researching. Methodism had a strong hold here then you know – John Wesley – an excellent man, but sadly mistaken in many ways. Now could you be doing something with them, Sister?'

'You mean repairing them?'

'You being an artist so to speak. Could they not be cleaned up?'

'Depending on what was used. Pencil might – but these seem to be done in ink. I can take them away with me and test a couple, Father. I'd have to tell Mother David of course.'

'Ah yes, the new prioress! Sister Dorothy rang me to inform me. Of course you must, Sister, but the nearer we can keep this to ourselves the better.'

'You say the cupboard was locked?'

'Oh yes.'

'Where is the key kept?'

'On my keyring.'

'There's no spare key?'

'There might be. One usually has a spare key made for fear of losing the original. I couldn't swear there is one.'

'And the church is locked at night?'

'Last thing. It's a sad necessity with the crime wave soaring out of sight. You heard about Mrs Pearson?'

'Seeing what she thought was *the* or *a* devil? Yes.'

'Some nasty piece of work trying to frighten an old lady.'

'She thought it real enough.'

'Well, moonlight can play tricks. It's a sad world, Sister.'

'In many ways, yes,' she said sombrely.

'But we must look on the bright side!' He locked the now empty cupboard and rooted around for a folder in another drawer. 'Here we are! I'd not want the other dear sisters to see them! You will do what you can?'

'Yes, of course, but I can't promise complete success,' she warned. 'Drawing and painting are not the same as restoring manuscripts. You'd do better to put the whole thing in the hands of an expert.'

'Which would only spread the infection,' he said gloomily. 'No. You do your best, Sister. One cannot ask more than that!'

Infection. The word stayed in her mind as she drove away.

An unusual term to describe a spot of rather nasty vandalism but – infection?

It was past lunchtime, a fact she glumly checked on her watch before she carried the shopping inside.

'Detective Inspector Mill rang from the station,' Sister Marie said, pausing briefly in the washing-up. 'He told Mother David about Alice and that you might be delayed. He said you were leaving her at the vet's. How on earth did she get on to the quay?'

'Wandered away probably,' Sister Joan said. 'Will you excuse me, Sister? I need to see Mother David.'

'There's some lunch for you if you haven't eaten. I made a potato gratin with the rest of the cheese since you couldn't get the groceries here on time,' Sister Marie said brightly. 'We shall have salad sandwiches for supper as a nice change. I saved you some of the gratin.'

'That was kind, Sister. First I must speak to Mother David.'

Extracting the folder from the rest of the shopping she headed for the parlour.

'*Dominus vobiscum.*'

It might have been Sister Dorothy seated behind the desk so alike were the alert posture and level intonation of the customary greeting.

'*Et cum spiritu sancto.*'

Sister Joan kissed the floor in token of unpunctuality and seated herself.

'Did it take you the whole morning to check on Alice?' Mother David enquired.

'No, Mother Prioress, but Father Malone wished to see me.'

As well not to mention her call upon Mrs Pearson.

'Oh?' Mother David adjusted her spectacles, looking rather like an inquisitive little owl and less like the rabbit Sister Joan imagined her resembling.

'He wants me to do what I can about these. I shall need your permission.'

She leaned forward and laid the folder on the desk. Mother

David took it up slowly, slid out the documents and visibly blenched.

'What happened, Sister?' When she raised her head her visage was subdued, almost grieving.

'They were kept in a locked cupboard because of their historic value,' Sister Joan explained. 'Father Malone went to the drawer and found them in this state. I might be able to remove the – er – sketches.'

'You have my permission. Why did Father go to the cupboard?'

'He didn't say, Mother. I think he had an idea that he ought to check on them in case Rome showed an interest.'

'And he has the only key?'

'He believes so, Mother, but of course a duplicate key might have been made.'

'The cupboard wasn't forced then?'

'Not as far as I could tell,' Sister Joan said.

'Is it possible that he left the cupboard unlocked on a previous occasion? He has so many duties that he might well have neglected to check properly.'

'It's possible.'

'What does Father Stephen make of it?'

'He's still on his working holiday.'

'And Sister Jerome?'

'Her day off. Father Malone had only just discovered the – vandalism. He spotted the van and rushed out.'

'You must be wanting some lunch, Sister. Fortunately Sister Marie rustled up something very tasty and kept some back for you. You may eat it in the refectory.'

'And the documents?'

'You may do what you can to minimize the damage, Sister. Leave them with me. I shall take them up to the library and secure them. I am only sorry we two were forced to see them.'

'Yes, Mother. Oh, I had—'

'Please don't tell me how many cups of tea you have drunk this morning.' There was a glint of amusement behind the round spectacles. 'I am in no condition to receive fresh shocks.'

'Thank you, Mother. *Dominus*—'

'You say Father Stephen is still on his holiday?'

'Yes, Mother. He's writing a paper on church murals. Why?'

'Here and there. . . .' Mother David bent her head over the documents again. 'Father Stephen makes rather elaborate capitals with a reverse loop on the g and the y. There are similar reverse loops on the – er body parts of these unspeakable sketches. Probably a coincidence. *Dominus vobiscum.*'

'*Et cum spiritu sancto*,' Sister Joan said numbly.

A coincidence. Yes, it had to be a coincidence. Sister Joan got herself out of the parlour and stood for a moment in the antechamber, fighting an unaccustomed wave of depression that swept over her like fetid water.

A couple of days before, she mused fretfully, the most exciting thing on the horizons of convent life had been renting out the postulancy and the election of the new prioress. Then a series of isolated incidents had changed life's perspectives – or were they isolated? Was there some link between Alice shivering on the quay and the loops on a lewd sketch?

'Am I to take your lunch up to the refectory or will you be having it with me in the kitchen?' Sister Marie enquired, coming out with a covered tray.

'Mother Prioress suggested the refectory. I can carry it, Sister.'

Relinquishing the tray, Sister Marie shot the other a worried look.

'You look all of a doodah, Sister,' she said. 'Are you sure Alice is going to be all right?'

'Positive! I've had a bit of a busy morning, that's all,' Sister Joan said.

The refectory opened on to the wide landing at the top of the beautifully carved staircase, and led thence into the recreation-room.

It too bore traces of former glory in its panelled walls and polished wooden floor. A long table and stools and a low side-board now comprised its furnishings. By rights the refectory would be more conveniently situated on the ground floor since the older members of the community were finding it increasingly difficult to struggle up the stairs, but to have suggested they eat in the infirmary would have hurt their pride.

She applied herself to the warmed over potato gratin to which Sister Marie had thoughtfully added an extra layer of hot cheese and drank the accompanying cup of tea.

In her mind disparate events revolved uneasily. The painted obscenity under the sink in the postulancy, Alice's escapade, Mrs Pearson seeing a devil, the defaced books in the postulancy and the documents in the locked cupboard of the church sacristy.

Were they connected or simply random events that occurred by chance around the same time? Not necessarily the same time, she thought. There was no knowing exactly when the books had been despoiled and the ugly word painted in the tiny kitchen. Father Malone, she guessed, had probably not looked at the old documents for months.

But who had access to the church and the postulancy? Who, for example, could have been cavorting around in the grave-yard a couple of evenings before? As far as she could recall all the sisters had, as usual been indoors. Or had they? Sister Marie had been excused from recreation in order to help Sister Hilaria pack up some things in the postulancy. She had seen Brother Cuthbert emerging from the postulancy. Was he in the habit of wandering around the unlocked building?

Groundless suspicions were useless! She finished her meal and walked through to the recreation-room. Its long, elegantly sashed windows looked out over the enclosure with its fruit trees, flower bushes and the neat rows of vegetables that were Sister Martha's pride and joy.

There was no Sister Martha to be seen, only the ungainly figure of Luther as he squatted, head bent over something he was digging with a small trowel.

'Sister Joan! Mother David wishes to see us in the parlour!'

Sister Dorothy, two purple ribbons adorning her sleeve, had come in.

'Is something wrong?' Sister Joan asked.

'Goodness me, I have no idea,' Sister Dorothy said, reverting briefly to her previous position of authority. 'We had better hurry on down. Have you finished your lunch? No, I'll take the tray.'

Sister Joan hastened. At some point she would have to tell Sister Dorothy, in the latter's new capacity as librarian, that she was doing some restoration work on some old documents, but for the moment that would have to wait.

Mother David looked pleased and slightly excited as the sisters filed in. She hadn't yet grown into her position, Sister Joan thought with a flash of sympathy. Prioresses were calm and concise, seldom betraying emotion. Mother David was beaming.

'I have just received excellent news, Sisters,' she said without preamble. 'I have received a letter from a Father John Fitzgerald in Liverpool. Sent express. It concerns the renting out of the postulancy.'

'We have prospective tenants?' Sister Hilaria sounded slightly nonplussed. 'Nothing is really ready, Mother David.'

'A lady called Mrs Winifred Roye,' Mother David said, referring to the letter before her, 'is anxious to move to Cornwall following the death of her husband last year. She lives with her married daughter and son-in-law who will be accompanying her. Apparently the son-in-law, a Mr Ian Lurgan was recently made redundant and hopes to find work down here. He has, Father Fitzgerald informs me, several likely interviews to attend. They are Catholics – though I didn't specify any tenants should be – but being of the Faith they will be more likely to understand the rules of semi-enclosure and keep to their own part of the grounds.'

'When do they want to come?' Sister Perpetua asked.

'In two weeks' time. They have only personal possessions,

no furniture. We must make a list of essential items to be purchased.'

'There are already beds there,' Sister Hilaria said.

'Husbands and wives usually have double beds,' Sister Gabrielle remarked, 'unless customs have changed since my youth.'

'Thank you, Sister. I believe we are all aware of that,' Mother David said.

'And a cot.' Sister Katherine spoke dreamily.

'No children are mentioned,' Mother David said.

'I only thought – after the double bed?' Sister Katherine's delicate features were bright red.

'Sister Joan, you had better help me draw up a list and then we can calculate cost,' Mother David said. 'Sister Dorothy, your advice would be invaluable in this matter. I have decided to accept Father Fitzgerald's recommendation and write to inform him we shall expect Mrs Roye and Mr and Mrs Lurgan in a fortnight's time. I think we're all agreed this is very welcome news.'

There was a general chorus of assent before the customary farewell. In the hall again Sister Joan found herself hesitating. She ought to start on the documents, she supposed, and give Sister Dorothy some hint of what it was all about, but she felt disinclined to cloister herself up in the library.

Instead she went through the kitchen, paused to promise Lilith a ride later, and strolled round to the vegetable garden. There was no sign of Luther but the hole he had been digging was neatly filled in.

It was hardly the time for planting anything, she thought. The earth had been smoothed over but one could easily see its ruffled edges. Frowning slightly, she knelt and began lifting out the impacted earth with her hands. As the sod came up with a slight sucking sound she looked down at the tiny bloodied corpses of two fledgings lying at the bottom of their blood-stained grave.

Suddenly she felt sick and dizzy, but before the feeling had passed she was hastily filling in the hole again.

FOUR

'Sister Joan! Sister Joan!'

Checking Lilith in her canter Sister Joan waved to the two schoolgirls who were walking up the track towards her.

'Tabitha, Edith, how are you both?'

At fifteen Tabitha Lee was developing the contours of a young woman; her twelve-year-old sister was as skinny and dark as usual.

'We've both gone up a year,' Tabitha said.

'I've got Miss Montgomery,' Edith intoned mournfully. 'She's ever so strict.'

'It won't do you any harm,' Tabitha said, in a motherly way. She had been mother to Edith since the death of Mrs Lee two years before. On the other hand, Sister Joan reminded herself, their father had for most of their lives acted in both parental capacities since the late Mrs Lee had been partial to a drop or two.

'You haven't been to the camp for weeks and weeks,' Edith said on a complaining note.

'I've been very busy,' Sister Joan excused herself. 'Tell your dad that I'll be over soon. Is he well?'

'There's been a bit of bother,' Tabitha confided.

'What kind of bother?'

If Padraic had been caught poaching then she and the other

49

sisters were guilty by association since most of the salmon he filched ended up in the convent kitchen.

'One of our lurchers was poisoned,' Edith broke in. 'Arsenic or summat. Dad was proper upset about that. He said if we saw you we were to ask after Alice. Is she better?'

'She came home more than a week ago,' Sister Joan said. 'Inspector Mill was kind enough to bring her.'

'Sergeant Petrie told Dad that someone tied her up down on the old quay,' Tabitha put in.

'Happily she wasn't badly hurt,' Sister Joan said. 'I'm sorry about your dog though.'

'He was pretty old,' Edith said. 'Not too quick at the rabbiting.'

'Which doesn't give anyone the right to poison him,' Sister Joan said.

'We'd best get on!' Tabitha tugged at her sibling's sleeve. 'Dad gets fussed if we hang about after we get off the school bus.'

'That's because he doesn't want you running off with the lads!' Edith said cheekily, wriggling free and dashing off across the moor.

Sister Joan waved to them again and turned Lilith's head for home. She would ride over to the camp the next opportunity that arose and commiserate with Padraic over the loss of his dog. Meanwhile she missed the cheerful presence of Alice bounding along at the pony's side. The dog was quite recovered from her slight injury but the vet had decreed a rest for a couple of weeks, so Alice now reclined in a basket in the kitchen and sucked up shamelessly to Sister Marie, purveyor of titbits.

There had been little opportunity for her to talk with Alan Mill when he had brought Alice back. Not that she was in the habit of seeking his company she reminded herself. Special friendships, especially with members of the laity, were largely discouraged. But she would have liked to ask him if Mrs Pearson had reported any further sightings of a demonic figure, or if anything else untoward had occurred in the town.

Half an hour before religious studies! Time galloped faster than Lilith!

She was just stabling the pony, giving her the customary rubdown, when Mother David came out into the yard, shivering as the autumn wind caught her habit and blew her skirts sideways.

'Sister Joan, have you time to go over to the postulancy?' she asked.

'Yes, of course, Mother. Is anything wrong?'

'Nothing at all as far as I know,' Mother David said. 'With our tenants moving in after the weekend I want to check that everything is correct – locks and bolts, furniture in place etcetera. Sister Marie and Sister Katherine will be hanging up the curtains tomorrow. Sister Katherine has chosen a particularly pleasant shade of blue to go with the rugs. And see if you can spot Luther anywhere.'

'Doesn't Sister Martha—?'

'Sister Martha has a nasty cold so Sister Perpetua has ordered her to remain indoors by the infirmary fire for a few days. The main work in the garden is drawing to a close anyway though there are still berries to be picked. Luther hasn't been around much this past week or more. Of course, he's completely unpaid for the help he gives but that can't be the reason. Sister Martha says he has seemed out of sorts for some time.'

'Yes,' Sister Joan said thoughtfully.

'Well, off you go then!' Mother David gave an impatient little jerk of her head and made for the kitchen door again.

Though it was still full daylight there were streaks of an early twilight in the sky and the wind was increasing, winding itself in gusts through the shrubbery. The garden had a melancholy air, dahlias shedding dead petals on to the soil and windfalls from the apple trees littering the grass. She wished suddenly that she had Alice with her as she traversed the shrubbery and went down the steps and across the old tennis court.

The keys! She'd forgotten to ask for the new keys that now rendered the postulancy secure. Reaching the front door, newly painted a gleaming white, she bit her lip in exasperation.

The front door opened and Brother Cuthbert emerged, so exactly in the same manner as he had done on the previous occasion that she had seen him here that she had the sensation of time slipping backward.

'You've come for the keys, I daresay, Sister,' he said in his amiable fashion. 'I came over earlier to pick up the books for Sister Hilaria and she gave me the keys.'

'Books?' Sister Joan said stupidly.

'There were some books in the library. She forgot to take them when she picked up her things. I was on my way over to ask after Alice when I saw her so I offered to run down for her but they seem to have gone.'

Carted away with the rest of the rubbish and incinerated. Sister Joan said aloud, 'I think they must have been mislaid, Brother Cuthbert. They weren't of any particular value, were they?'

'Oh, I don't imagine so. Not in monetary terms anyway. I was just thinking how strange it will be to have tenants here and not see Sister Hilaria with her charges coming to and fro from the convent.'

'Brother Cuthbert, there aren't any postulants or novices left for the time being,' she said. 'Vocations are very scarce these days. We couldn't leave Sister Hilaria to rattle round here all by herself! And the Order needs the money.'

'Yes, I had heard.' His blue eyes were slightly bewildered as he fixed them on her. 'I don't pretend to understand it at all you know! The religious life is so thrilling! I tell you I sometimes feel quite guilty when I wake up in the morning. I mean this is supposed to be a life of sacrifice and the truth is there's no sacrifice to speak of at all!'

'You don't think so?' she queried.

'You know I once thought that I'd like to be a priest,' he was continuing. 'Now don't laugh but I used to quite fancy the idea of being before the altar or in the pulpit! Fortunately my tutor at the seminary set me straight. "You are a natural reclusive," he told me. A nice way of letting me know that I was too absent-minded to run a parish! Not to mention all those church laws and indulgences and *ex cathedra* statements to bear in mind. And he was right, bless him! I pray for him every day. That's one thing I never forget!'

'I have to check the locks,' Sister Joan remembered.

'Then I won't keep you. God bless you and all who come to live here!'

He strode off, whistling, his habit and cowl flapping in the wind.

Going inside, Sister Joan had a moment of confusion. The local workmen had more than come up to scratch. The whitewashed walls gleamed, the polished wooden floors were laid with blue rugs, and the unblocked fireplaces in the downstairs rooms were laid with wood and coal ready for the cold weather. The connecting doors between the two lecture-rooms had been removed to create a curtained arch, the curtains so far not hung, which resulted in a large sitting-room. There were a couch and four armchairs, a bookcase and a couple of coffee tables there now instead of the blackboards and wooden seats.

At the other side of the narrow passageway the tiny kitchen had been similarly extended into the old library to provide a kitchen cum dining-room with a wood-burning stove in the old fireplace, a table and four dining-chairs and a spanking new oven, refrigerator and washing-machine set against one wall and the former bookshelves filled with cheap but cheerful pieces of crockery.

She tested that the windows were locked and the back door and set her foot on the lowest rung of the staircase.

Over her head sounded a sharp crack as if someone had

stepped on a loose floorboard.

For a moment she felt a chill of apprehension. Then her usual common sense took over and she called up the stairs.

'Hello! Is anyone there?'

A moment's aching silence and then footsteps.

'Is he gone then?' a voice enquired.

'Luther? What the devil are you doing here?' she exclaimed. 'You frightened me out of my wits!'

She was already running up the stairs, the jeans she wore under her habit when she exercised Lilith, rendering her ascent more modest than it otherwise might have been.

'I never done nothing!' Luther said, emerging from one of the former cells. 'I never done nothing to Sister Martha.'

'No, of course you haven't.' Sister Joan stared at the unkempt figure before her. 'Why should anybody think you'd done anything to Sister Martha?'

'I heard Sister Marie say as how she was in the infirmary,' he gabbled.

'Sister Martha has a cold and is merely sitting by the fire in the infirmary,' Sister Joan said. 'Why are you here anyway? Mother David told me that you hadn't been yourself this last week.'

'And I never killed them baby birds neither,' Luther said. 'I couldn't never do summat so bad as that, Sister! They were special, late hatching long after others had flown. I was tending them gentle like for the parent birds had flown or been killed I reckon.'

'You found them dead and buried them. That's it, isn't it?'

She stepped into the nearest cell, now a small but attractive bedroom with a single bed, chest of drawers and narrow wardrobe and stared at him.

'All broken and bloody,' he said mournfully.

'But why didn't you—? You didn't want Sister Martha to see them? That's it, isn't it?'

'Sister Martha be that tender with living things, plant or bird,' Luther said.

54

'And it troubled you greatly. Luther, you ought to have told someone what had happened. Nobody would think of blaming you!'

'One of the Roms told me that Cousin Lee's dog were poisoned,' he said. 'And someone took Alice. Best to lie low when bad things happen.'

'Padraic's lurcher may have picked up something acciden-tallly and Alice probably decided to wander off,' Sister Joan said, not believing it herself. 'Whatever happened there's no sense in hiding away! Anyway our new tenants will be here after the weekend. You can't stay here.'

'I never slept on them beds,' he assured her.

'No, of course you didn't. Now let me check the locks up here and then we can walk back together.'

She went past him into the bathroom and looked at the window there with its close mesh. No mirror of course. The tenants would certainly expect a mirror.

The two cells next to the bathroom had also been restored into one large room containing now a wardrobe and double bed. She wondered vaguely how the men had got it up the stairs and checked the neat pile of sheets and duvets – duvets for heaven's sake! Now who had thought of those?

On the other side next to the small bedroom the two remaining cells had also been knocked into one. There was a single bed here and a put-you-up settee. Almost everything was in readiness.

When she went downstairs again there was no sign of Luther. He had, she reckoned, probably scooted off to the camp. She hoped her own reassurances had relieved his mind, but with Luther one never knew.

She put her hand in her pocket for the keys and grimaced. Brother Cuthbert had walked off with them! Between Luther and Brother Cuthbert, she thought crossly, there sometimes were many resemblances!

She was already late for religious study. In for a penny! Closing the front door behind her she set off at a run towards the convent, arriving panting in the parlour just as Sister Perpetua was extolling the virtues of moderation in eating and drinking.

'*Dominus vobiscum*,' Mother David said wearily.

'*Et cum spiritu*, Mother David – and I went without the keys,' Sister Joan said.

'You didn't get them from Sister Hilaria?'

'No, Mother.'

'But of course you didn't know she had them!' Mother David said, twitching her snub nose irritably. 'I ought to have remembered myself so I am just as much at fault as you!'

'I gave them to Brother Cuthbert,' Sister Hilaria said, her tone faintly surprised. 'I cannot recall why – something to do with books.'

'There is a second set here in the drawer.' Mother David slid it open and brought them out. 'Not that we shall have the right to use them once the tenants are here. I ought to have given them to you in the first place! You had best go over and lock up securely at once. It would be too unfortunate if there were to be trespassers in the postulancy now that nearly everything is ready. You are excused religious studies for today. *Dominus vobiscum*.'

'*Et cum spiritu tuo*.' Sister Joan went out more slowly than she had entered.

It was growing perceptibly darker, the wind rising to toss the bushes this way and that as if some force strove to uproot them, and overhead incoming clouds scraped the darkening sky with claws of murky purple and rust.

She would have liked to take Alice but Alice was still limping slightly, purely to gain sympathy Sister Joan guessed, but the early evening was dwindling too rapidly towards night for her to leave the warm kitchen.

Instead she took her cloak from its peg in the antechamber and let herself through the front door, the keys firmly clutched in her hand.

There had been a time before she had joined the Order

when the sisters had worn grey habits to their ankles and tight white linen caps under their coifs. The sixties had introduced modernization, with habits rising to mid calf, caps abandoned and short grey veils edged with white.

'Making us,' Sister Gabrielle had snorted, 'look like district nurses!'

In a cold, blustery wind it would have been cosier to have been more closely covered, she thought, hugging her cloak about herself as she hurried along the side of the shrubbery towards the postulancy.

The last fragile rays of day illumined the uncurtained windows of the building as she went across the tennis court.

No, not daylight but candlelight! She stopped short, squinting against the eddies of dust blown up from the concrete and stared at the little flickering lights.

She could turn and run back to ask for a companion. Or she could stop behaving like a fool and find out what was going on. The electricity and the water were both operational so if anyone had arrived ahead of time there was no need for candles.

She opened the front door and went in, deliberately shutting it behind her with a bang. Nothing stirred but a candle placed on the floor in a tin sconce waved wildly before the flame sank to a splutter.

She bent and picked it up, blowing on it softly until it flamed up again and went into the newly adapted sitting-room where the lecture rooms had been. There were candles set in sconces here, two on the window sills at each end of the apartment, others on the mantelshelf. When she stepped across the passage into the kitchen-diner she saw more candles, all freshly lit and scarcely burnt down at all.

There had been a large box of candles in the cupboard under the sink. She bent to open the door, half dreading what she might see, but the box still in its neatly sealed plastic jacket was still there. In any case, she reminded herself, these had been plain white candles, whereas the ones illuminating the rooms were coloured. Black and dark green, she noted, and thickset with ridges curling around them.

She hesitated, silently accusing herself of cowardice before marching firmly, candle in hand, up the uncarpeted stairs.

Here was darkness. No candle save the one she held burned. She glanced briefly in each room, then went downstairs again.

And why was she pottering about with a candle when the electricity was on? Her hand moved to a switch and hovered uncertainly.

Electric lights blazing forth would certainly signal her presence. Instead she went into the lower rooms, extinguished the candles and having provided herself with a bucket from the kitchen stuck the smoking columns of coloured wax into the two inches of water at the bottom. They sizzled, giving off a pungent smell that made her feel slightly giddy as sometimes happened when Father Stephen swung the censor too energetically before High Mass.

But these were not church candles. They were clumsily made, home-made perhaps. There was no point in speculating. Instead she locked the back door, locked the front door, the last remaining candle in her hand blown out by the wind as she did so, and with the bucket on her arm began her trudge back to the convent.

She would stick the candles in one of the refuse bins, she decided, put the bucket in the stable and return it when she had an opportunity.

If she didn't make haste she would be late for chapel and for benediction too. Then she could wave goodbye to any recreation for several days.

Stumbling over a root she bent down wincingly as the swinging bucket caught her on the ankle.

At precisely the same instant something landed on her shoulder, digging in sharp claws.

'Ah-ah!' She couldn't avoid a startled yelp before the creature leapt down and streaked away again.

58

'Malkin!' Instinctively she called out the name and the large cat paused in its flight to stare at her from its emerald eyes before it continued its flight. Mrs Pearson! The name wrote itself across her mind as she rubbed her ankle, grateful for the thick stockings she wore.

Mrs Pearson had walked a long way, she reflected grimly, in order to light the evil-smelling candles. It was highly unlikely that her cat would have wandered up here alone at the precise time someone else was making mischief in the postulancy.

'Mrs Pearson! Mrs Pearson!' Finding her voice she raised it against the wind.

There was no answer. Sister Joan resisted the temptation to take the same direction as the cat and, promising herself that she would call on the old lady as soon as possible, went on towards the convent.

First there were the candles to dispose of. She lugged the bucket round to the refuse bins and lifted the lid of one, her heart contracting in panic as another hand was laid on her arm.

'What?'

Swinging round violently she saw a familiar countenance beaming at her in the dusk.

'Can I give you a hand with anything, Sister?' he enquired genially.

'You frightened me half to death!' she gasped.

'I'm awfully sorry! The wind's pretty noisy so it probably muffled any sound I made,' he said apologetically.

'Brother Cuthbert, what are you doing here?' she asked shakily.

'I walked off with the keys,' he said. 'I really am getting quite absent-minded these days. Do you want me to go and lock up the old postulancy for you first?'

'All done and dusted! Mother Prioress had another set in her desk.'

'And I could have saved you the trouble—' he began.

'Do forgive me, Brother Cuthbert, but I must go and make ready for benediction,' she broke in.

'I'm so sorry, Sister! I'll leave you to get on then!'

'If you go into the kitchen Sister Marie will likely make you a quick cup of tea,' Sister Joan said, putting on the lid of the refuse bin and beginning to regret her shortness of tone.

'And Father Malone will shortly be on his way! No, thank you, Sister. I have some meditating to do before I retire tonight. I shall be sorry to miss benediction though. What a delight it always is!'

'Then stay for it. Father can give you a lift back when it's over.'

'Next week perhaps. I need a good long windy walk to clear my head,' he said.

'It's certainly windy,' she agreed.

'A cleansing wind with healing rain to follow, please God. My regards to the Sisters.'

'Brother Cuthbert—?'

'Yes.' He turned back in mid stride.

'The keys?' she said.

'Oh, good Lord!' He dug in his pocket and handed them over.

'I'll see that Mother gets them,' she said. 'Are you sure you won't—'

'I have to get back. Be safe, Sister!'

He trod the grass silently in his sandals. Safe from what, she wondered, as she carried the now empty bucket round to the stable?

FIVE

Sleeping in the cell that opened on to the kitchen had its advantages, Sister Joan thought. Though it meant trudging upstairs to one of the two bathrooms there to take her turn in the queue for water it meant that being so near the cooking area the cell itself always felt slightly warm. It also meant that she could whisk out to tend Lilith and let Alice out before the latter forgot she was supposed to be trained and disgraced herself on the matting.

Even the fact that it was Saturday which meant confessing one's sins before the assembled sisterhood didn't distract from the pleasure of waking up feeling reasonably warm. Not, she thought as she dressed, that one could claim to be completely warm at five o'clock on a dull, dark morning! She had woken once or twice during the night to listen to the wind as it wailed about the building and the occasional gusts of rain that threw themselves against the shuttered windows.

In chapel, the flickering candles reminded her uneasily of the strange black and green candles she had found in the postulancy. The memory of their sweetish yet acrid smell and of Malkin's claws digging into her shoulder was disquieting. With determination, she settled herself to the private devotions which occupied the time until Mass.

Sister Hilaria rose and went into the sacristy as a car was heard drawing up outside the door. It was something of a disappointment when, instead of the homely features of Father

Malone, Father Stephen's chiselled profile was seen as he stepped up to the altar.

He was back from his working holiday then. She ought to be glad, she reminded herself, that his return would lighten the burden on Father Malone who must be past sixty yet never stinted his efforts, but the truth was that the mellow tones of the younger priest, the slightly theatrical manner in which he elevated the Host, the whisper of his beautifully worked robes as he moved about served only to irritate her. Certainly she could never have envisaged confiding her present worries to him.

At breakfast, as they stood eating their bread and apples and drinking their coffee, he was full of his recent trip to Rome.

'Of course many of the older murals are quite badly faded but I'm happy to say that concentrated restoration work is being done on them and from my own small stock of knowledge I was able once or twice to point them in the right direction,' he was saying.

'I've always wished,' Sister Perpetua said unexpectedly, 'that the camera was invented centuries ago. How marvellous it would be to have a photograph of the Blessed Virgin.'

'We might be disappointed,' Sister Joan heard herself say. 'She was never blonde and blue-eyed for a start!'

'It is how we picture her mentally that matters,' Father Stephen said. 'There may have been blonde tints in her hair.'

'Father, she came from Northern Israel!' Sister Joan said with a throb of impatience in her tone. 'Brown or olive-skinned with dark eyes and dark hair – I will grant you a tinge of red in the hair since she was of the line of David and that tribe often had reddish hair, but not fair!'

'We are all indebted to Sister Joan for her information,' Father Stephen said, a trifle too graciously. 'Mother David, I've not yet congratulated you on your elevation to the position of prioress.'

Sister Joan clenched her teeth and bit into the core of her

apple. Luke would've had some sarcastic remark to fling back, but Luke, being Jewish, had scant regard for clergy of any denomination, including his own.

Why did she suddenly think of Luke now after long years of not thinking of him? It was so long since she had seen him that if she were to meet him now she probably wouldn't recognize him. In the old days, both at art college, he had been lean and dark and intense, forcing her to query every assumption she held. Refusing to marry him had been the sharpest pain she had ever borne. Now it was no more than a faint ache in the recesses of her being – the vague recollection of a pain that had passed more than anything else.

She shook off the depression that threatened to descend on her and, by way of contrition but feeling a bit of a hypocrite, asked Father Stephen if they would be permitted to house a copy of his published paper on Renaissance murals in the library.

'After His Lordship the Bishop and Father Malone you shall be the first to receive a copy, Sisters!' he assured her.

'Sister Joan, I have been thinking,' Mother David said, as he took his leave and they began to repair to their cells to clean them before going to their various duties, 'that it might be a pleasant gesture if we were to stock up the refrigerator and the cupboard in readiness for our tenants when they arrive on Monday. Could you drive into town this morning? Sister Marie will give you a list.'

In the kitchen, Alice, having contemplated the outside world through the back door, decided to remain convalescent for a little longer and curled up in her basket again.

'Cereal, long life milk, sliced bread, some frozen hamburgers – we can't expect them to be vegetarians – tea, coffee, sugar, eggs – potatoes and cabbage and fruit and some jam we can spare from our own stocks,' Sister Marie said. 'I'm going to help Sister Katherine put up the curtains there today. Oh, and a nice bottle of wine if the money stretches that far.'

'I'll see to it. Oh, Mother David now has two sets of keys,'

Sister Joan remembered to tell her.

Sister Joan went off briskly, shivering slightly as the wind caught her. It was more like March than September, she thought, as she climbed up into the vehicle. In the van it was comparatively warm. She switched on the engine, let in the clutch and drove towards the track that led her past the little schoolhouse where Brother Cuthbert now lodged and into town.

As she had half expected, Brother Cuthbert was outside, his arms full of broken branches from the fringe of trees that outlined the level ground on which the former schoolhouse stood.

'The wind brings blessings as well as discomfort!' he said, as she drew up. 'Luther and I shall have a fine fire tonight.'

'Luther's with you? Thank goodness, I had begun to wonder where he'd vanished!' she exclaimed.

'He's rather disturbed at present, poor chap!' Brother Cuthbert allowed a faint frown to cloud his cheerful countenance. 'Fretting about Sister Martha and her cold – is she better?'

'Much improved.'

'I shall tell him so. He went over to the camp earlier to see Padraic Lee, Dreadful about the poor lurcher!'

'Yes indeed. Was there anything you wanted from town?'

'I've everything I need right here,' he said simply. 'Drive carefully, Sister Joan!'

'I will!'

She raised her hand in salute and continued on her way. At least Luther would be all right. Brother Cuthbert wouldn't ask questions or pry into what had upset him but go calmly and joyfully about his work and contrive to find the silver lining behind every cloud.

The stray thought that living with such unrelenting good humour would drive her crazy made her smile for a moment.

She parked neatly and legally, went into the supermarket and bought the required supplies.

When she emerged it was to see Mrs Pearson standing by the door of the coffee shop attached to the store, a flapping mackintosh covering her brightly knitted coat, a hat plonked firmly on her head.

'Sister Joan, isn't it? We met—'

Her nose was tipped with red from the chill of the wind and her eyes were red rimmed from what Sister Joan guessed might be another cause.

'Mrs Pearson, how are you?'

There was no answering smile. Mrs Pearson clutched at her arm and said in a hurried whisper, 'You haven't seen him, have you?'

'The Dev— who exactly do you mean?' Sister Joan corrected herself.

'Malkin, my cat. He didn't come home last night,' Mrs Pearson said.

'You let him out? When?'

'Late afternoon. It was getting quite dark and the wind was starting up. I thought he might want to do his – excuse me, Sister – his tiddles before the rain started, though it seems to have died down.'

'And he didn't come home?'

'I went out to look for him,' Mrs Pearson said. 'I walked up on to the heath and quite a long way – the wind drove me on and I was quite worried you see. Malkin doesn't like wet weather.'

'Did you go as far as the convent grounds?'

'Almost as far but the wind was really very rough and I had no torch with me so I turned back. I thought I heard mewing but he was nowhere to be seen. So I turned round and went home again. I've been awake half the night hoping he'd come home. I always leave the pantry window open a little way. There's still no sign of him.'

'I was over at the postulancy – that's the smaller building on the edge of the property round about four-thirty – five o'clock. I saw your cat then. He streaked off.'

'It must've been around six when I reached the moor,' Mrs Pearson said in a troubled tone. 'You didn't see which way he went?'

'No, I'm sorry. Perhaps he ran past you as you were on your way?'

'But he'd've come to me even in the dark,' the other fretted.

'Perhaps the wind upset his sense of direction? I only caught a glimpse of him. Were you wanting anything particular here?'

'I thought I might put an advertisement in – the woman in the coffee shop often puts them in the window.'

'If I were you,' Sister Joan said, 'I'd go home first. Malkin may well be waiting for you there.'

'Do you think so?' Worried eyes peered through the drizzle. 'You don't think – if the forces of evil had got him!'

'Mrs Pearson . . .' Sister Joan hesitated, then rushed on, 'I do think, living by yourself as you do, it isn't very sensible to read about such things. They must disturb the imagination. I'm sure that Father Malone would tell you the same thing.'

'But the Devil does walk—'

'You saw someone dressed up to frighten peoople. Surely the actual Devil has better things to do than cavort in a church-yard with only one witness to see him and take fright?'

She had spoken to no avail. Mrs Pearson dropped her hand and shook her head in a hopeless way. 'He is legion,' she said, in a breathless mutter and, turning, hurried away before Sister Joan could reply.

The wind seemed to blow her out of sight.

She gripped her own packages more securely and, ignoring the scent of fresh coffee drifting through the café door, went back to where the van was parked.

This evening was general confession. One extra unlicensed tea or coffee would mean more hours on her knees than she had time to spare.

By the time she was halfway back to the convent she was

66

regretting her brusqueness. Mrs Pearson might be a trifle – more than a trifle – eccentric, but she deserved better than a brush off. If she could find some excuse to drive into town later she'd pay the old lady a call.

She parked outside the enclosure wall and carried the bags of groceries to the postulancy. The new curtains were almost all up, their cheerfulness removing the last traces of bleakness from the building.

'Oh, you've brought the stuff! That's kind of you, Sister!' Sister Katherine emerged, smiling as she relieved the newcomer of her burdens.

'What do you think?' Sister Marie was on the stairs.

'I think they look really pretty,' Sister Joan said, 'but won't they get damp with all the windows open?'

'Oh, I shall be closing them in a few minutes,' Sister Marie said cheerfully. 'It was the smell actually.'

'The smell?'

'I don't know what it was. Kind of sickly and sweet and yet acrid at the same time. It certainly wasn't here when I was a postulant.'

Sister Marie, who was all of twenty-seven, spoke as if she was recalling a time almost lost to memory.

'You haven't seen a cat anywhere around?' Sister Joan asked.

'No. Is there a stray about?' Sister Katherine wanted to know.

'An old lady in town seems to have lost hers. Name of Malkin – the cat, not the old lady.'

Both nuns shook their heads.

Leaving the groceries, she got back in the van and drove round to the front gates which always stood open.

'Mother David wants to see you,' Sister Dorothy said, as she passed her in the hall. 'Something to do with the books she's writing.'

'In the parlour?'

'She's up in the library. She asked me to itemize this

month's bills for her. Then she can start with everything in order.'

'Right, Sister.'

Sister Dorothy inclined her head slightly and went on into the parlour. It must feel strange, Sister Joan mused, to go back and sit at a desk behind which one has dispensed authority for ten years. Did Sister Dorothy regret the rules that had demoted her, or was she content to fill the not very demanding post of librarian?

The library itself was over the chapel, a large square room reached by a flight of circular steps behind the Lady Altar. On the other side of the narrow landing were two storerooms filled with the boxes and discarded furniture of more than fifty years.

'You wanted to see me, Mother Prioress?'

Mother David, bent over a table, looked more at home here than in the parlour.

'Have you made any progress on the spoiled documents?' she asked.

When, thought Sister Joan, have I had any time? Aloud, she said placatingly, 'Not yet, Mother.'

'I have been looking at them,' Mother David said. 'Not a very pleasant task I fear, but I believe the – obscenities were made with a ball-point pen. I wondered if, with bleach and a fine brush, it might be possible to eradicate them without spoiling the paper. What do you think?'

She moved aside to enable the other to examine the document placed in the glare of the table lamp.

'The paper is certainly thick,' Sister Joan agreed. 'It would certainly be possible to get rid of the . . . marks though it might roughen the surface of the paper itself. I can certainly try.'

'If you take them into the further store-room – I've placed a table and chair there and a lamp, though on a brighter day the skylight will provide sufficient illumination. Make a start anyway. I know that Father Malone is anxious to have them back safely.'

'Of course, Mother. About the books – when did you want me to make a start on the illustrations for them?'

'Hardly books, Sister!' But Sister Joan had caught the quick flush of pleasure on Mother David's face. 'Booklets really – easy for a child to hold. I have the first five here. Saints Anne, Bernadette, Christopher, David and Elizabeth. You may get on with the illustrations whenever it is possible for you to do so without neglecting your religious observances, or any other duties you may have.'

'Thank you, Mother Prioress.'

It would be a treat to use her talent again – talent and not genius – she reminded herself. There were times when between carrying out odd jobs, driving into town, exercising Lilith, she wondered exactly what function she might be said to play in the life of the Order.

She worked away steadily with the bleach and the paint brush relieved to find that the disgusting little sketches had been only lightly sketched in. Father Malone would certainly be relieved though she personally doubted if he would ever be required to render them up for the inspection of Rome!

After lunch, as they rose from the table, Sister Perpetua said, 'What's all this about a cat? Sister Katherine told me that one was lost.'

'An elderly lady in the town – a Mrs Pearson – has lost her cat and is rather distressed about it,' Sister Joan said.

'The animals locally do seem to be having rather a bad time of it,' Sister Dorothy remarked, frowning slightly. 'First Alice wanders away and hurts her paw, and then someone mentioned that one of Padraic Lee's lurchers had been poisoned—'

'And those late fledgings I was telling you about,' Sister Martha said, voice still husky with cold, 'seem to have taken wing and flown. I do pray they had the strength to manage the long migration.'

'And now a cat has gone missing,' Sister Dorothy said. 'Do we know this Mrs Pearson, Sister Joan?'

'She's a widow – her husband died – ten years ago I believe. No children, so her cat is probably her constant companion. I believe she's one of Father Malone's parishioners.'

'It always fills me with amazement,' Sister Gabrielle said, 'to realize how knowledgeable Sister Joan is about the local laity!'

'Someone has to keep us in touch with the outside world,' Sister Dorothy said, unexpectedly defensive.

'Surely we are here to escape from the outside world,' Sister Mary Concepta said, in her gentle, elderly voice. 'For my own part I thank God for the security of the religious life every day!'

'But you've been here for centuries!' Sister Marie said tactlessly.

'Not precisely centuries, Sister dear.' The old lady's blue eyes were faintly reproving. 'I entered the religious life in 1932. This Order had not then been founded of course, but I joined the Carmelites. I was with them for nearly twenty years but the austerity of the Rule was too much for my health. So I received permission to transfer.'

'Didn't I read somewhere that you also entered in that year?' Sister Katherine enquired of Sister Gabrielle.

'The Sisters of Mercy,' Sister Gabrielle said. 'I transferred to the Daughters of Compassion as soon as Rome gave permission.'

'So Carmel and the Sisters of Mercy lost two fine sisters and we gained two,' Sister Hilaria said.

'Mind you,' Sister Gabrielle said with a thump of her stick, 'if I'd known I'd spend my declining years cooped up in the infirmary with Mary Concepta here and a dog called Alice I might've thought twice about it!'

It obviously being meant as a joke they all laughed.

'I think,' said Mother David, 'we had better all get back to our duties.'

Which meant an afternoon working with the bleach and the little paintbrush, Sister Joan thought. She was anxious to get on with the task so that she could the sooner start on the illustrations. She had taken a few moments to glance through the little pile of carefully typed booklets before going to lunch and been pleasurably surprised. Mother David had written in a clear, lively style with pleasant little touches of humour that would appeal to young children, and the touches of piety weren't laid on with too heavy a hand.

This being Saturday, benediction would be followed by general confession. She reminded herself to mention the extra cups of tea and after carefully laying the documents she had repaired in a drawer where they could dry out of sight she went downstairs in time to see Sister Marie on her way up.

'Did you want me, Sister?' she asked.

'Lilith is making a bit of a fuss in her stable,' Sister Marie said. 'Mother David asks if you have time to exercise her.'

On Saturdays there was no hour of religious studies since with the greneral confession looming, the sisters were to spend time contemplating their faults and the faults of their companions – not a process she enjoyed – and in writing up their spiritual diaries. Exercising a restless pony was not exactly in that category. On the other hand the wind had dropped and the dusk was held at bay by a marvellous sunset.

'I'll take her out at once,' she said. 'Thank you for telling me, Sister Marie.'

In her cell she wriggled into the jeans she had been given leave to wear when on horseback, pulled on her cloak and went out. Alice set up a hopeful whine but she hardened her heart, shut the kitchen door and went to the stable.

It took only a few minutes to saddle the pony and mount, Lilith immediately straining forward in her lust for exercise.

'Let's blow the cobwebs out, old girl!' Sister Joan said. She was clear of the convent grounds and trotting across the open moorland within a few moments more. She had set her course westward into the sunset with the intention of fulfilling her promise to visit the Romany camp.

The camp itself occupied level ground next to a river that burbled down from the higher ground and provided water for the occupants of the vardos and lorries pitched roughly in a semicircle.

Already Padraic was striding to meet her, his dark face set in a look of intense concentration.

'Thought you might come, Sister.' He helped her down and stood back regarding her with a definite frown.

'You're cross because I haven't been over for a while? I do have other duties,' she began.

'It's not you that troubles me, Sister,' he said.

'Not Tabitha and Ed—?'

'Nay!' His face broke into an involuntary smile. 'I tell you, Sister, them girls be a real blessing to me! Getting on fine at school too. Mind, they'd you to teach them proper before the damned council closed the little school!'

'Thus giving Brother Cuthbert a place to stay,' she reminded him.

'Aye, that's true, right enough.'

'And I was sorry to hear about your dog. It was poison?'

'Fed to the poor beast by someone. I'd like to feed them the same when I catch 'em,' he said darkly. 'Old Nell were in the way of wandering a bit – too old for the rabbiting but a good old maid for all that. No, someone gave her summat – arsenic most like the vet told me. T'other dog's being kept close to my vardo till they find the one killed Nell.'

'Well, as long as the rest of you are all right—' she began.

'Things ain't right,' he said firmly. 'There's evil come.'

'Oh, but surely—'

'Evil,' he repeated. 'Old Sara feels it. "Keep your girls close when they'm not in school" old Sarah said. I was coming over soon with fish for your larder but the fishing went clean out of my head when I saw the poor animal.'

'Your dog?'

'Nay, a cat. Not that I've much use for cats,' he admitted. 'Companions for witches if you ask me! But this one was a fine, sleek beast—'

'A tawny cat?'

'Aye, marked like a tiger. Drowned dead in the river just beyond the old cemetery. Tied to a bag of stones and tossed in I reckon. I landed it with my rod – thought it were a salmon or summat until I jerked it clear of the water. Bloody incomers!'

'Was there – did it have a collar on?' She had a vague recollection of one.

'Aye, a leather one with M on it in brass or some shiny metal. Anyways I gave it a decent burial.'

'I'm sure you did the right thing,' Sister Joan said vaguely. 'If you'll excuse me now I have to get on!'

Blindly she turned, gripping the reins, hearing her own voice crack with misery.

'Sister Joan—?'

'Another time, Padraic. Any fish will be very welcome!'

She left him standing in perplexity and swerved eastward, setting Lilith at a gallop over the moor.

Lights were casting neon glares over portions of the narrow streets as she slowed to a canter and then a trot. The drowned cat had to be Malkin. It had to be! But why would anyone want to do something so cruel to a harmless animal? And if Mrs Pearson had heard about it, what might that do to her state of mind?

This time she went to the front door of the cottage and rapped sharply with the knocker, leaving her mount loosely tethered to the iron railings that fenced off the minute front garden from the road.

There was no answer but she could see light coming from an upper window. Mrs Pearson might be ill, shocked by the loss of her pet, or worrying herself sick about it if she hadn't heard the news.

She turned and ran down the back alley, pushed open the yard door and went across to the back door. Bolted! What had Mrs Pearson said about the pantry window? She left it open for Malkin to go in and out.

The window was open. She pushed up the sash and legged

it over the sill, pushed open the door facing her and found herself in the kitchen.

'Mrs Pearson! Don't be alarmed! It's only me, Sister Jo—!'

She could smell the sickly sweet, acrid fumes of the candles as she ran up the narrow stairs and flung open the first door she came upon. Candles, livid green and dull black, set in saucers and makeshift sconces were burning in the bedroom, one on the window sill, one on the dressing-table, one at each side of the double bed on which Mrs Pearson lay.

She was wearing a dressing-gown as bright as her knitted coat and her eyes were open, filmed over slightly but open. There was, at first horrified glance, no way to determine exactly how she had died.

SIX

There was also no point in touching her, in closing those wide blurred eyes, in covering the stark white face with its partly open mouth.

Nobody at the convent possessed a mobile phone. Sister Dorothy when prioress had made her feelings quite clear on that point.

'Unless one is a policeman or a doctor there is absolutely no necessity for anyone to be constantly at anyone else's beck and call. These machines are a gross invasion of privacy – useful possibly on occasions of extreme emergency, but otherwise simply an excuse to spread gossip as fast as possible.'

At this moment Sister Joan wished she had one. The smell of the candles was making her feel sick and the staring eyes seemed when she glanced again to have hardened in their fixed regard.

She backed slowly towards the door, pulled it wider with one hand behind her, went down the narrow stairs and into the kitchen. It was neat and tidy, a cup and saucer upended on the draining board, a tea towel folded on a chair on top of a low pile of newspapers.

It would be stupid to go out through the pantry window and

thus destroy further traces of whoever had made their entrance that way before her own arrival. She slid the bolt back on the back door and went across the little yard and into the alley. There was a telephone kiosk further along where the alley joined the street.

The telephone itself had been wrenched out and hung limply at the end of its cord. Torn up bits of the directory littered the floor.

Vandals! She bit back an exclamation that would certainly have shocked her fellow religious and stood irresolutely for a moment. She could of course walk to the station which was only a couple of streets away but distaste for leaving Lilith tethered outside the cottage determined a different course of action. If anyone thought it peculiar to see a nun riding a pony through the streets just as dusk was threatening they must lead far too sheltered a life.

She was filling her head with irrelevancies because the image of the old lady, of those squat, ridged candles, of the open eyes, had joined into a single picture that disfigured the landscape of her mind.

' 'Evening, Sister. We don't often see you out after tea time.'

'Sergeant Petrie!'

His measured tread, his cheerful voice, the familiar uniform of the law banished horror. She went across to him swiftly.

'Sergeant, do you have a mobile phone? – oh, but of course you have!'

'What's wrong, Sister?'

'I've just found Mrs Pearson dead,' she said rapidly. 'She's lying on her bed and – something terrible has happened to her. Can you get hold of something to—?'

For some insane reason she had been going to say 'cover her eyes'.

'Inspector Mill is still in his office, catching up on a bit of paperwork,' Sergeant Petrie said. 'You sit here on this bit of wall and I'll get through to him. You're sure she's dead?'

'Quite sure.'

'And not – natural?'

'Not natural,' she repeated, her voice shaking. Despite her cloak she felt cold and shivery.

He stepped a few paces away and spoke into his mobile. Perched on a bit of broken wall she controlled her shivering with an effort.

'Inspector Mill says can you wait here while he rings the convent?' Sergeant Petrie was asking. 'Seeing as you found the body and all.'

'Yes, of course.' She answered quietly, the thudding of her heart reverting to its normal regular rhythm. She had seen death before in more shocking guises but there had been an almost palpable sense of horror in that candlelit room.

A sudden plaintive whinny roused her from her thoughts.

'Excuse me, I'd better see to Lilith,' she said, rising and making her way along the road to the front gate.

'You came to see Mrs Pearson then?' Sergeant Petrie said.

'On impulse. I went over to the camp and met Padraic who told me that he'd found a cat – a tawny cat – drowned in the river. I guessed it was Malkin, Mrs Pearson's pet, when he told me that it had on a collar with the initial M on it. I was out exercising Lilith so I decided to ride into town and break the news to her myself.'

'And the front door was open?'

'No. At first I thought she might be out, still looking for Malkin, and then I saw the bedroom was illuminated so I – well, I climbed in through the pantry window. She always left it open for her cat.'

She flushed slightly as the possible charge of trespass flashed into her mind.

'And went upstairs,' Sergeant Petrie said without emphasis.

'Yes. I felt – suddenly uneasy. It was most irregular of me.'

'Here comes the inspector,' he said, as a car nosed into the street. 'I'll just quickly fill him in on what you've told me.'

Alan Mill alighted from the car and stood for a moment or two, dark head bent as he listened intently.

'You've no keys to the house, Sister?' His tone was formal.

'Sorry about the pantry window,' she muttered.

'An unconventional means of entry but you were worried. Can we get in through the back door, Petrie?'

'I came out through the back door,' she volunteered. 'It's closed but not locked. It was bolted before.'

'It was bolted before?'

'Yes.'

'Right, well go in that way. I rang the hospital. They're sending someone down who, I hope, can tell us whether we need to treat it as a police matter.'

'But surely—' she began.

'Old ladies have been known to fall asleep and not wake up again,' he said briefly, leading the way down the alley. 'Unless she's been under medical supervision very recently there'll have to be a post-mortem of course. What did you touch, Sister?'

'The front railing where I tethered Lilith, the front door knocker. I could see light coming from the upper front window and that's why I became slightly concerned. I went round, opened the door leading into the alley, knocked on the back door and then remembered she left the pantry window open for her cat to go in and out.'

'If it's necessary we can take your prints,' he said. 'Right! We'd better check first that she is—'

'She is quite certainly dead,' Sister Joan said levelly.

'In the front bedroom. Right! Yes, come with us.'

He stood aside and she went as briskly as her reluctance would allow up the stairs.

'Was the door open when you came upstairs?' he enquired.

'Closed – yes, closed. I left it open when I came out again.'

'Odd smell!' Sergeant Petrie commented. 'She didn't use hash by any chance?'

'I'd think it very unlikely.'

She tried to speak lightly, to avoid the staring eyes of the small figure in the brightly patterned dressing-gown on the bed, head propped on its pillow.

Both policemen had slipped on transparent gloves. She stood by the door watching as Alan Mill went over to the bed, bent to listen, shook his head slightly as he straightened up again.

'Nothing on her lips, no corrosion,' he said. 'The doctor will be able to tell us more.'

He moved to lift a corner of the dressing-gown.

'Almost fully dressed.' He let the flap of the gown fall into place again. 'Slip and skirt, stockings, no shoes.'

'Shoes are here, sir.' Sergeant Petrie pointed to a pair set neatly side by side

'It looks as if she came upstairs for a lie down,' Alan Mill said. 'You hadn't been in this room before, Sister?'

'I only visited her once,' Sister Joan said. 'Well, not exactly visited. I came down to see the place where you found Alice tied up. Then I realized that Mrs Pearson, the old lady who reported she'd seen the Devil, lived here. I was wondering whether or not to call – sometimes lonely people imagine things you know – and then the cat – Malkin – jumped out at me and she came out and invited me in – through the kitchen into the sitting-room. I stayed for a cup of tea and then I left.'

'What impression did you get?' He asked it as seriously as if she'd been a colleague.

'That she read too much about the occult,' Sister Joan said frankly. 'I mean there's nothing intrinsically wrong about the occult – the word only means hidden after all, but everything has its dark side. A susceptible person, living alone except for a cat, might not have the mental strength or the knowledge to distinguish between the two. They might easily be fooled by some nasty practical joker into thinking they'd seen the Devil in a churchyard.'

'Do you still think that?'

'I think it's more than a practical joker,' she said slowly.

'Things have been happening recently – small things, not in themselves important perhaps save to the people they most nearly concern, but nasty, spiteful things – the lurcher poisoned, Alice lured away – she has never wandered off of her own accord, the fledgings—'

'What fledgings?'

Briefly she told him about the birds.

'You don't think Luther—' Sergeant Petrie queried.

'No, not Luther! He's harmless, wouldn't hurt anyone or anything. Someone else sneaked in and killed them. Luther buried them to save Sister Martha from being upset.'

'There's another thing on your mind,' Inspector Mill said. It wasn't a question.

She thought of the spoiled books in the postulancy, of the documents that Father Malone had wanted repaired. Though those incidents were not under any seal of the confessional she would require Mother David's permission before she mentioned them.

'The candles here,' she said at last. 'Last evening I had to go over to the postulancy – I must stop calling it that now we are to have tenants living there! – anyway I went over to check the place – you know it is often left unlocked.'

'Sister Hilaria,' Sergeant Petrie said.

'Whoever. When I got there candles were burning in nearly every room – candles exactly like these. There was the same odd smell. I took them all up and was on my way back to the main house when the cat, Malkin, leapt out of the shrubbery on to my shoulder. He streaked off again at once. Mrs Pearson told me that Malkin had strayed away. She was going to put an advertisement in the café window. I told her that I'd glimpsed Malkin near the postulancy. She did say she'd walked that way earlier but then turned back.'

'Did you mention the candles you'd seen burning?'

'No.' She shook her head. 'The truth is that I half thought she might've put them there herself.'

'Why?'

80

'Oh, I don't know. Perhaps when her story about seeing the Devil in the churchyard wasn't taken seriously, she decided to stage something else up in the postulancy in a bid to convince people she'd been speaking the truth.'

'Did she know the postulancy was empty?'

'She could have done. Father Malone might've mentioned that the place had been rented out.'

'A very long way for her to walk,' Sergeant Petrie said.

'She wasn't infirm,' Sister Joan said. 'And she could've had a lift. Some of the Romanies drive their trucks up on to the moor after the week's buying and selling is completed.'

She jumped nervously as the sound of a car drawing up outside was followed by the sharp rat-tat of the front door knocker.

'That'll be the doctor now. We'd better go down. He's a new man, very competent as far as I've heard – done some good forensic work over at Truro.'

She walked down the stairs rapidly, glad to be out of the room, to breathe purer air instead of the sweet, dizzying smoke curling up from the half burned-out candles.

The man who came in was in his late thirties, fair hair receding from a high forehead, nod brisk and impersonal as he said, 'Apologies for the delay. I was in the middle of a tricky experiment that couldn't be left. You say an elderly woman has died?'

'Mrs Pearson. She wasn't by any chance a patient of yours? Oh, this is Sister Joan from the Daughters of Compassion. Dr Metcalf is a new addition to the local hospital staff.'

'Sister!' He gave her a brief, unsmiling glance before turning towards the inspector again. 'Where is the woman?'

'Upstairs. Sergeant Petrie will show you. We've touched as little as possible.'

'Not my concern,' Dr Metcalf said. 'That's for you lot if you think it's necessary. Oh, and no, she wasn't a patient of mine. I checked on the hospital computer before I came out.'

He followed Sergeant Petrie up the stairs, his briefcase held tightly in one hand.

'I'll have forensics in anyway just in case,' Alan Mill said. 'Look, I can run you back to the convent in my car.'

'I have Lilith,' she began.

'We'll put Lilith up at the station overnight and I'll have her brought back in the morning.'

'But I really can't expect—'

'Us to keep acting as your unofficial boarding kennels cum stables? Don't worry about it. I'll have Constable Seldon come over for her. She's a keen rider.'

She? That must be the young naturally blonde policewoman she had seen typing away in the office.

'Thank you,' she said meekly.

He opened the front door again to let her pass him. Outside, the wind still tossed the grass verges on the road and sent small stones tumbling down the slope of the intervening alleys.

'Seat belt,' he said automatically, as she got into the car.

'I was going,' she said, 'to fasten it.'

'So, any ideas, Sister?'

She shook her head.

'Not really. It just seems so odd that Mrs Pearson should die now at this time. And the candles—'

'What did you do with the ones you found in the postulancy?'

'I put them in the refuse bin,' she admitted.

'That's not like you,' he said mildly.

'Look, Alan' – she turned her head towards him as he drove along the moorland track – 'right now there's a lot going on at the convent. We've a newly elected prioress who has to settle into the position though really she's doing very well. Money's tight which is why we're renting out the postulancy – and while the money will be useful, being able to rent it out at all means that fewer women are entering the religious life. And all kinds of nasty little things have been happening –

Alice was lured away. I know she was! And Padraic Lee's lurcher was poisoned. She wasn't a young puppy who might've picked up something by mistake. She was an old dog. And then there was Mrs Pearson insisting she'd seen the Devil or a devil in the churchyard. I think she did see someone who was trying to frighten her. And two late fledgings were killed – battered to death in the enclosure garden. Luther found them and buried them in case Sister Martha saw them. I haven't said anything about them to anyone else. There were other things, but I shall need Mother David's leave before I can tell you.'

He was silent for a moment, frowning slightly as he drove along the track towards the open gates of the convent. Then he said, 'I'd appreciate it if you obtained that permission from Mother David fairly soon. Unless it ties in with anything it would be kept quite confidential I promise.'

'And Mrs Pearson?'

'They'll be taking her to the hospital as soon as Dr Metcalf has completed his preliminary examination. We should get the results through by tomorrow. I'll let you know as soon as I know. I've a feeling there won't be any prints anywhere around apart from yours and the old lady's.'

'The candles? That smell?'

'Will be analysed too. Here comes Sister Marie!'

The younger nun was hurrying round from the back of the building, undisguised relief on her face when she saw Sister Joan in the glare of the headlights as the latter emerged from the car.

'Oh, thank goodness you're all right!' she exclaimed. 'Did Lilith throw you? Surely not! Mother David said to keep supper warm for you if you were late but it's only just ready. Padraic stopped by with some fish.'

'Salmon?'

Inspector Mill had alighted from the car.

'Trout,' Sister Marie said. 'We're having them with butter sauce and mashed potatoes. Where is Lilith?'

'Lilith's fine. They're keeping her overnight down at the station,' Sister Joan said.

'Mother David said an elderly lady had died down in the town. How very sad,' Sister Marie said.

Her voice was completely sincere as she blessed herself but her round, rosy face was ill made for expressing grief.

'Yes. Very sad,' Sister Joan said.

'I'm forgetting my manners!' Sister Marie said. 'Will you come in for a cup of tea or coffee, Inspector?'

'That's kind of you but I'm still on duty,' Alan Mill said.

'I always think that policemen must be most dedicated people,' she was continuing. 'All those hours, and having a family too! How is your family? And the boys?'

'The boys are back at boarding-school,' he said politely. 'And Mrs Mill is very well.'

Her name was Samantha, Sister Joan knew, but only once had she heard him refer to her by her Christian name. And they had never met. He kept no comfortably familiar family photograph on his desk.

'Sister Marie,' she interposed gently, 'hadn't we better go in?'

'Yes, of course. Oh Lord, my potatoes!' Sister Marie whisked kitchenwards.

'Thank you for the lift,' Sister Joan said. 'Look, tomorrow's Sunday. Could you possibly keep Lilith until Monday if it's not too much trouble? Only Sunday is High Mass and then private prayer for most of the day.'

'We'll board her for the rest of the weekend. And what exactly will you be doing for the rest of this evening?'

'After supper we have general confession,' she said, somewhat disconcerted by the question. 'We confess to one another instead of one of the priests and the prioress gives out the penances. We can do them at once or delay them until tomorrow. There's no recreation, but one of the sisters reads from the Bible or some devotional book. Why do you ask?'

'I was wondering why you didn't get more vocations,' he said drily. 'I think I begin to see why now. Good night, Sister Joan.'

SEVEN

'We must certainly acquaint Detective Inspector Mill with all the facts,' Mother David said thoughtfully. 'Whether all the recent incidents are connected or not everything must be brought to his attention. Sister, why did you say nothing about the despoiled books and the oddly perfumed candles?'

'I saw no point in upsetting anyone,' Sister Joan said, uncomfortably.

'You could have come privately to me.'

'I just felt that it would be too upsetting.'

'So you presumed to judge my reaction to what was at the least upsetting evidence that there are vandals about – and vandals of a rather vicious nature? You also destroyed evidence.'

'I apologize, Mother Prioress,' Sister Joan said. 'At the time it seemed like the most sensible course of action.'

'At the very least you should have reported it to me.' Mother David spoke mildly enough but her eyes behind her spectacles were cold.

'I apologize again,' Sister Joan said. 'I used my own judgement and I was wrong.'

'At least you acquainted me with all the facts this morning,' Mother David said with a small inclination of the head. 'In future, Sister, instead of acting independently it might serve you and the rest of us better if you refrained from behaving as if you had special privileges in this community. I am not suggesting you rush round telling everybody when anything out of the ordinary happens but I do suggest you think very hard before you take independent action again. Is that clear?'

'Yes, Mother.'

'At least you had the common sense not to blurt everything out in general confession. You may regard our talk here as fulfilling that obligation. If anything else occurs I shall expect to be told. I hope that's clear?'

'Yes, Mother Prioress.'

'Then you had better walk down to the gate to await Lilith. I received a telephone call this morning that the police were bringing her back at ten o'clock.'

'Will you want to see Inspector Mill if he comes?' Sister Joan asked.

'No. If he has any relevant information concerning the death of that poor lady then you will of course tell me. *Dominus vobiscum.*'

'*Et cum spiritu sancto,*' Sister Joan said with relief, and got herself out of the parlour.

Mother David had been correct of course. She did use her own judgement too often, assert her own small measure of independence.

She bit her lip, called Alice who came bounding out, forgetting the slightly theatrical limp with which she had prolonged her convalescence and walked down towards the gates just as the police car with Sergeant Petrie riding Lilith alongside came into view.

'Good morning, Sister Joan.' Sergeant Petrie slid from the saddle.

'Good morning. Thank you for bringing Lilith back.'

'I'll take her round to the stable for you, shall I?' he went on cheerfully, leaving Alice in a dilemma whether to stay where she was or trot after him.

'Off you go!' Sister Joan resolved the problem with a wave of her hand and waited for Inspector Mill to turn the vehicle around and get out of it.

'Mother David is occupied,' she said, 'so if you have anything to report I am to inform her.'

'Only your prints where you said you'd left them. Of course we shall have to check that they are your prints. Is it possible for you to come down to the station this afternoon?'

'I'm due to meet the tenants for the old postulancy at three. They're coming by train. I could probably come at two-thirty?'

'Just a process of elimination. We won't find any other prints.'

'They wore gloves?'

'Nobody wore gloves,' he said.

'But Mrs Pearson—?'

'Mrs Pearson died of a heart attack. Dr Metcalf phoned from the hospital. She'd been receiving medication for angina for some time. She went as an out-patient so he had no reason to see her. Apparently it's rare for the mild angina she had to develop into a full blown heart attack but last night – late afternoon apparently, she felt ill, went upstairs to lie down and died before she could get help. There was no telephone in the cottage – unusual these days but since she had no family and kept herself to herself she probably viewed it as an unnecessary expense.'

'And the candles?'

'We found a stack of home-made candles, mainly green and black but also red and blue and brown in one of her kitchen cupboards.'

'But that's crazy!'

They had begun to stroll up the drive but she stopped short, indignant rejection in her face. 'Why would—?'

'You thought yourself Mrs Pearson might've put the candles in the old postulancy,' he reminded her. 'In fact we know now that she did. One of the gypsies called across to us as we were leaving the house yesterday to ask if the old lady was all right. He'd given her a lift up on to the moor a couple of nights back and she set off in the direction of the convent. He said she was carrying a fairly large bag with her. It clinked a bit when he handed it down to her and he supposed she was bringing some junk over for a bring and buy or something.'

'When was this? I mean what time?'

'Latish afternoon he said. If you remember it got dark quite early and there was a high wind.'

'When I went into the postulancy the candles had only just begun to burn down at all,' Sister Joan said. 'Did Mrs Pearson have her cat with her?'

'He said not. She told him the animal had strayed and she was fretted about it.'

'And he didn't give her a lift back?'

'No. Mind you, the walk back is a pretty long one even though it's downhill most of the way. Maybe that long walk in the wind and rain strained her heart.'

'I must've just missed her,' Sister Joan said.

'And the cat did startle you?'

'Yes, for an instant. It leapt away and – I suppose it set off down into the town again, but it never reached home.'

'Whatever happened it ended up in the river,' he said sombrely.

'And Mrs Pearson died.'

'Of a heart attack probably induced by overexertion and worry about her cat.'

'And there were prints where I recalled touching things in the cottage and – her prints too I suppose. Are you going to check the old postulancy because the tenants are arriving? It might make them uneasy to find police at the scene.'

'I doubt if it's necessary,' he said. 'Obviously for some wierd reason of her own she lit her home-made candles in the postulancy and then lit them in her bedroom.'

'If you're feeling the first symptoms of a heart attack then surely you don't start lighting candles. You lie down, take an aspirin—'

'She had been dead no more than an hour when the doctor saw her, probably less,' he broke in.

'I see.' She shook her head slightly to clear it of confusion.

'But she did light the candles?'

'Made them, set them in their sconces, lit them, then probably took off her top garments and lay down. What else is on
your mind?'

He had paused in their stroll, his eyes intent on her profile.
'Mother David,' she said carefully, 'feels you ought to know
that a couple – no, about three weeks ago, I found some books
in the library at the postulancy. I went over to take them to the
main house. They were religious books – popular lives of the
saints, that kind of thing, for the novices to read. They had
been scribbled over with obscenities, with nasty little drawings.
And under the sink in the little kitchen someone had painted a
four letter word on the wall.'

'What word?'

'Shit,' she said reluctantly.

'Pretty mild in today's world,' he commented.

'Not in the convent enclosure!' she said with spirit. 'And the
words and pictures scribbled inside the books were foul
anywhere.'

'What did you do?'

'I painted the bit of wall under the sink to obliterate the
word—'

'Don't tell me! You put the spoiled books in the refuse bin.'

'I'm afraid so,' she said ruefully. 'I didn't tell Mother David
about them or the candles until this morning. Oh, and Father
Malone had some historic documents in the sacristy – old
baptismal certificates from the eighteenth century. He found
the drawer where he kept them locked up, unlocked and the
documents drawn and written over – fortunately lightly so
we've been able to get the marks out. I did tell Mother David
about that at once. It was before I found the books.'

'Did Father Malone know how long they'd been missing?'

She shook her head.

'I gathered he takes a look at them occasionally. He probably hopes that one day Rome will send for them. He had his
key with him but there may have been a second key made. If

so he doesn't know where it is. Or he may have simply forgotten to lock the drawer the last time he looked at them and whoever sneaked into the sacristy found the drawer unlocked.'

'The sacristy itself being also unlocked I daresay?'

'The parish church is locked at midnight.'

'But people go in and out during the evening I suppose?'

'I would think so,' she said. 'People pop in to say a quiet prayer on their way home from work, or the ladies go in to arrange flowers, and there are confessions of course.'

'For contravening every known law of personal and property security give me a religious any time!'

'There's nothing valuable in the church in material terms,' she said earnestly. 'Even the documents have no more than curiosity value.'

'And, of course, nobody troubles to lock up the postulancy?'

'There's nothing there to steal,' she defended. 'And the odd local vandal isn't going to come all the way out here to despoil a wall and some books that few people are ever likely to see.'

'It sounds like someone with a grudge against the clergy,' he said musingly. 'I suppose it's no use asking you if there are liable to be any prints on the documents?'

'I used bleach. They were quite easy to clean.'

'And the books went in the refuse bin just ahead of the candles. Sister, these things ought to be reported!'

'I thought it best not to alarm anyone unnecessarily.'

'And you didn't see anyone hanging around the postulancy who had no right to be there?'

Brother Cuthbert had emerged twice from the building and Luther had been hiding there, she remembered.

'People from our Community go backwards and forwards all the time,' she evaded. 'We had the local builders here and the sisters have been in and out on various errands, but I can't see—'

'Did anyone supervise the builders?'

'Oh yes, one or other of us was always on hand. Anyway, why on earth would anyone working for a reputable local firm do such a thing? How could they with other people coming in and out?'

'Fair point. Mrs Pearson?'

'Because she set the candles round? Alan, the candles were lit. They were meant to be seen. The – word, the spoiled books and documents were done slyly – they might not have been noticed for ages. And that old lady was a nice old lady! She may have gone in and lit the candles but not with any ill intent, I'm sure.'

'You can find the mind's construction in the face, can you? Actually I'm inclined to agree with you,' he said. 'You'd better tell Mother David the death was a natural one, and that we're merely tidying up loose ends by taking your fingerprints.'

He was still speaking but her mind had skipped off at a tangent.

'Sister?'

They had almost reached the front door and he was looking at her questioningly.

'The candles themselves,' she said. 'They smelt funny.'

'Sickly sweet, a mite acrid at the same time? They did.'

'Could you get them analysed? I mean, if there was anything in them which might have caused—'

'That's being done. Probably some hash mixed in with the beeswax – if we have the results by two-thirty I'll let you know. Sergeant!'

He raised his voice slightly just as the latter came from the direction of the yard.

'Lilith and Alice are having a chinwag,' Sergeant Petrie said with a grin.

'I wish animals could talk then Alice would be able to tell us who tied her up at the quayside,' Sister Joan regretted. 'Excuse me.'

She went in and tapped on the parlour door.

'And that seems to be that, Mother.' Ten minutes later she finished her recital. 'Mrs Pearson died of a heart attack and she put the candles in the postulancy and in her own room just before she died. Inspector Mill wants to take my fingerprints simply for elimination purposes though he doubts if the vandals left any prints anyway. May I call in before I meet the train?'

'Of course. There's no need to go to the other extreme and start asking permission for everything,' Mother David said, not quite smiling. 'Tell me, have you had an opportunity to glance through the books yet?'

'Indeed I have,' Sister Joan said. 'I think they're charming and I love the little touches of humour. I shall get down to some sketching tomorrow. I thought I'd make St Anne a nice, rosy grandmother type, maybe building bricks with the Child Jesus?'

'That sounds splendid.' Mother David had recovered her good humour completely. 'I wouldn't want you to neglect any other duties you might have of course but if we can raise money for the Order—'

'I shall fit everything in,' Sister Joan promised.

Shortly after two, she was driving the van over the moors in the direction of the town. Brother Cuthbert was chopping wood outside the old schoolhouse and straightened up to greet her.

'Always busy, Sister? You make me feel quite idle!' He shouldered the axe and came to the side of the van.

'I doubt if anyone could accuse you of that, Brother Cuthbert. You've a good big pile there,' she commented.

'Well, autumn's running towards winter and we might get a sharp one,' he said. 'Not that winter isn't a bracing time but a bit too bracing for some of the older Sisters I can't help thinking.'

'And no central heating,' Sister Joan said.

The Tarquins who had originally owned the estate had seen no reason to make the lives of their staff more comfortable. There would have been log fires blazing in the principal family rooms, she thought with a touch of envy. Since the Order had taken over the property there were fires only in the kitchen and the infirmary.

'Central heating does something nasty to the ozone layer,' Brother Cuthbert said unexpectedly. 'Not that I pretend to understand what that means exactly. Will the tenants at the old postulancy be requiring wood?'

'It would be a kindness if you could leave some logs in the little shed at the back door,' she nodded. 'I wondered – do you often walk over that way?'

'Hardly ever.' He seemed faintly surprised at her question. 'If Sister Hilaria ever needed anything and then the other day I went over to volunteer a hand with the alterations, but the builders made a good job of everything so Sister tells me.'

'It will seem odd for you not to be going there occasionally now that we have tenants – except for delivering the wood, that is.'

'Oh, I don't suppose I will be walking in that direction now once I've filled the shed,' he said. 'Excuse me, Sister. I'd better get on.'

Turning away he braced his sandalled feet apart and swung the axe again.

Muscular Christianity, Sister Joan thought. As the log split in a rending sound she raised her voice slightly,

'Is Luther still staying with you?'

'On and off. He's no trouble.' He turned back to answer her. Tiny slivers of wood chippings clung to his aureole of red hair.

'Tell him that Sister Martha is quite recovered from her cold and wants to start on preparing the ground for winter.'

'I'll tell him. Sister.' It seemed that he hesitated an instant before he continued, 'Luther told me about the fledgings.'

'Sister Martha doesn't know,' she said quickly. 'It certainly wasn't Luther who—'

'No. Luther wouldn't do that. Nor poison a lurcher, or drown a cat.'

'You know about that?'

'Padraic Lee told Luther about it and Luther told me. There's evil in such actions, Sister. Real evil.'

95

He turned, raising the axe again, sending it crashing through the wood, wood chips flying up. There was something resolute in the set of his broad shoulders.

'Well, God bless!' she said brightly, rather at a loss.

'As ever, Sister.'

He turned again and she saw in the wing mirror that he stood looking after her as she drove down the hill.

In the police station she found herself confronting the young blonde policewoman she had seen typing on her previous visit.

'Sister Joan, isn't it?' The girl looked like an actress dressed in uniform, her hair smoothed back from a pretty, expertly painted face.

'You're new here, aren't you?' she said.

'WPC Melanie Seldon. I finished my training three months ago and was posted here.'

'From?'

'Plymouth. I wanted a job in Cornwall. A bit of independence from the family. If you'd like to come through, Sister – Inspector Mill is up at the laboratory and Sergeant Petrie's got the afternoon off.'

'It's my fingerprints I've come to give—'

'Yes.' The girl shot her a cool glance. 'I was instructed.'

New and unused to dealing with the public, especially nuns, Sister Joan concluded, following her meekly.

'The prints will be destroyed of course,' Constable Seldon was saying a few minutes later as Sister Joan wiped her fingers.

Sister Joan nodded.

'How do you like Cornwall?' she enquired.

'Very well so far. I'm concentrating on my job though the crime rate seems to be very low here.'

'It seems to have risen slightly in recent days,' Sister Joan said lightly. 'You heard about Padraic Lee's dog?'

'He didn't report it officially but I heard about it. Not a nice thing to do.'

'No,' Sister Joan said soberly. 'No, it wasn't.'

'And the cat that was drowned.' Constable Seldon seemed to be unbending slightly. 'I am not a great animal lover but cruelty cannot be allowed to go unchecked.'

'No indeed.'

'Well, that seems to be all, Sister.' It was a clear dismissal.

'There you are, Sister!'

To her relief Inspector Mill was coming in. He looked from one to the other with a slightly lifted eyebrow,

'Sister Joan has given her fingerprints, sir,' Constable Seldon said formally.

'Fine! Not that they'll prove anything but it's procedure. I just came from the hospital.'

'And?'

'The candles were made out of beeswax mixed with crushed garlic and asafoetida.'

'With what?' Sister Joan looked baffled.

'It's an extract from a herb apparently, much used in olden times for teething babies and puppies with distemper. Has a foul smell and an even fouler taste I should imagine.'

'But it's not poisonous?'

'Not unless one took a large overdose. And that goes for any medicine. Apparently its nickname is Devil's Piss.'

'Mrs Pearson was invoking the—? Surely not!'

'No idea. Perhaps she simply enjoyed unpleasant smells. I had a word with the local coroner. Since she was on medication there'll be no need for an inquest. She has no family left and as far as I can tell very few friends. I've put a seal on her cottage meanwhile. You might ask if you can come down in the next few days and help me go through her stuff. There might be a will somewhere.'

'Sir, surely as a member of the public—' Constable Seldon said, in a disapproving tone.

'Sister Joan's a mate,' he said easily. 'You'd best get off and meet your tenants now. And get leave to come over and help look through Mrs Pearson's things in the next day or two, will you?'

'Yes, of course. Thank you, Constable Seldon.'

Going through the door, aware of the disapproval of the pretty policewoman, she felt like smiling, but the words 'devil's piss' stuck too firmly in her mind for even mild humour to break through.

EIGHT

She had parked the van outside the small station and now, going on to the platform, she realized afresh that winter was almost upon them. The usual thin stream of tourists on their way to Truro or headed for more friendly beaches had diminished to one harassed young mother with a couple of toddlers in tow and a local businessman who folded his newspaper neatly as he alighted from the train and strolled off, relief at having escaped the office for a couple of hours writ large on his face.

The awaited tenants had left the train as quickly as if they feared it might rush off with them still aboard, and stood in a huddle of four surrounded by various cases, bags and shopping trolleys.

'Mrs Roye?' Sister Joan advanced, smiling, one hand outstretched. 'I'm Sister Joan from the Order of the Daughters of Compassion. I've been deputed to meet you and get you and your luggage up to the old postulancy. Did you have a comfortable journey?'

The hand she grasped was so plump that she felt as if her own slim fingers were being sucked into blancmange. The face turned up to her, its owner being seated on a large square case, was round and pasty as an uncooked bun into which someone had stuck two large raisins.

'Nice of you to come down, Sister.' The voice was low and pleasant.

'Well, I've the van outside so we can have you settled in a short time,' Sister Joan said, extricating her hand.

She had the abrupt irrational fear that Mrs Roye might try to lever herself up and fail, pulling herself on top of the bulging thighs above which a black skirt rose too high for decency.

Mrs Roye, however, struggled up alone, legs still planted apart, smoothed back rather pretty grey hair from a face devoid of wrinkles and said, 'Very good of you, Sister, to take the trouble. Dawn, look sharp! We've not got all day!'

The young woman who would before long – perhaps already had – turn into her mother gave Sister Joan a quick, shy glance out of eyes more like blackcurrants than raisins, and nudged the man standing next to her in the ribs.

'Give us a hand, Henry!' she ordered.

'I was,' said Sister Joan tentatively, 'only expecting three of you, unless—?'

Perhaps Mrs Roye had married again since the tenancy agreement had been signed. No, surely not! She was, despite the unlined skin, in her mid sixties while the man just addressed was in his late forties at the most, hair greying, chin jutting, height and breadth of shoulder hinting at vigour. Or was he the son-in-law? If so, he was years older than the daughter who looked to be in her late twenties, lips scarlet, hair pulled back from a round, pallid face, white blouse cut so low that a pair of rather grubby bra straps were revealed as she bent down.

'Mr del Marco is an old family friend,' Mrs Roye said. 'He came down for a week or two to help us settle in. That's all right, isn't it?'

There was a third albeit tiny bedroom, Sister Joan remembered. There was also some rule about subletting, but that would be Mother David's problem.

'I imagine so,' she said noncommitally. 'And this is—?'

The youth standing a little way off to the side turned his eyes from contemplation of the empty railway track and said in a curiously flat tone from which all emotion seemed to have been drained, 'I'm Ian Lurgan.'

'My husband,' Dawn said with a little giggle. 'Come and help me here, babe!'

He was obviously stronger than he looked, lifting the case with one hand, and looking expectantly at Sister Joan as if he needed her permission to move.

'Just follow me,' she said, more briskly than she intended, taking two of the smaller cases and heading for the exit.

Behind her the others followed, not talking, lugging the various pieces of luggage with them.

'If you put the stuff in the back of the van,' she invited, 'three can sit behind and there's another place at the front.'

If Mrs Roye chose the front seat she would threaten to overlay the gears, she thought wryly. Mrs Roye, however, flowed over two-thirds of the back seat, leaving barely room for her daughter to squeeze in beside her. Henry – or was his full name Henrico? – clambered in among the suitcases without a word.

She drove in the midst of a heavy breathing silence. All four were either dead tired or paralysed with shyness in the presence of a nun. Only as they bumped up the rough track did Mrs Roye say, 'Look, Dawn! Moorland!'

'Back of beyond more like,' Dawn said, and sniggered.

At her side, Ian Lurgan said in his colourless voice, 'Looks pretty.'

'Oh, in summer when the grass is greener and the heather is turning purple then it's beautiful,' Sister Joan said.

'Is there a bingo hall in the town?' Mrs Roye asked, as they drove past the main gates of the convent and skirted the outer walls of the enclosure.

'I've no idea,' Sister Joan said. 'I don't think so.'

'Pity. I like a bit of bingo,' Mrs Roye said.

They had reached the side gate beyond which the old building could be reached without crossing the tennis court or invading the enclosure proper. Sister Joan drew up and said brightly, 'Well, here we are!'

The leaden silence lasted for a few seconds more. Then Henry said in his accentless voice, 'Right, Ian! Let's get this stuff out. Do you have the keys?'

'Yes, of course.'

She took the bunch Mother David had given her out of her pocket. Mrs Roye leaned over the back of the driving seat and clamped sausage-like fingers around them.

'What part is ours?' she wanted to know, when she had oozed down from the vehicle.

'If you can make that side gate your main entrance,' Sister Joan said, 'and the old tennis court isn't used for anything. The steps at the far side lead up to the convent grounds. That's private.'

'Is this where they used to wall nuns up alive?' Dawn asked.

'Actually, it's not at all certain that anyone ever got walled up, in England anyway,' Sister Joan said crisply. 'It used to be the old Dower House where elderly members of the Tarquin family – they used to own the estate – retired. We used it for our novices after that.'

'Girls don't want to go into convents these days,' Mrs Roye said. 'Right! Let's take a look!'

She went ahead to unlock the front door, a shaft of afternoon sunlight cruelly focused on her unfortunate legs.

Sister Joan moved to help with the cases but was intercepted.

'You leave that to us men, Sister,' Ian Lurgan said.

'In that case,' Dawn said with an ugly bad-tempered note in her voice, 'I'm not carrying anything either!'

'You were never a man, darling,' Henry said with a wink.

'Nice of you to notice!' She gave him a sideways grin and went after Sister Joan towards the front door.

From the top of the stairs Mrs Roye called down,

'I'm taking the room on the left next to the bathroom,'

'But that's—!'

Sister Joan shut her mouth on the rest of the intended sentence. She had been going to say that was the room with the double bed in it, but it was none of her business how they arranged their sleeping quarters.

'I don't hold with constant sex,' Mrs Roye announced.

'I beg your—?' Sister Joan looked up at her.

'Constant sex,' Mrs Roye said, coming down the stairs again. 'Weakens the mind. If my Fred had listened he'd've been alive today. I'll take the room on the left; Henry can have the small room while he's staying and Dawn and Ian can take the room on the right. It's got a nice view.'

Also a single bed and a put-you-up sofa, Sister Joan thought. Not that other people's sexual habits were her business!

Dawn, leaning against the wall of the narrow hallway, was rolling a cigarette. Her eyes slewed towards Sister Joan and she pulled a face of exaggerated guilt.

'We can smoke?' she demanded.

'Yes, of course, but not in the enclosure.'

'Where we're not allowed to go anyway. Like being at school!'

'Stop showing yourself up!' Her mother was manoeuvring the various portions of her anatomy down the stairs. 'This is a lot better than Liverpool and the rent's dirt cheap. Go and make yourself useful.'

'Whatever.' Dawn shrugged and wandered outside again.

'Nice big sitting-room.' Mrs Roye had flowed into the converted lecture-rooms. 'Very comfy!'

'Well, I hope you'll soon feel at home here,' Sister Joan said, following her in as the others began carrying various boxes and cases up the stairs. 'As you can see there's no central heating, but the fires are laid ready for lighting and Brother Cuthbert has chopped extra wood and piled it in the shed at the back. At least he said he would.'

'I thought this was a convent,' Mrs Roye said.

'Well, it is, of course, but Brother Cuthbert has leave from his monastery to live in solitude up in the old schoolhouse. We passed it on the way up though you may not have noticed. He's a contemplative but not quite a hermit.'

'And the rest of you live in the convent?'

'Ten of us including myself. Well, twelve actually but Sister Teresa has taken leave of absence in order to care for her father and Sister Bernadette is in the mission field.'

'Not many of you then?'

'There are other Houses of the Order,' Sister Joan said.

'A lot of women all locked up together,' Mrs Roye said with a sudden chuckling laugh. 'As bad as constant sex!'

'Actually we do have other things on our minds,' Sister Joan said coldly. 'If you'll excuse me I need to be getting back. We have our own routines to which we try to keep whenever possible. Mother David will come over tomorrow morning just to see if there's anything else you need, or any questions you need to ask. I'm afraid there's no telephone installed.'

'We've mobiles.'

'Yes, of course. Most people have them these days. There isn't any television either but it's possible to hire one – as you can see it's fully wired.'

'We brought our own,' Mrs Roye said. 'Don't you fret about us, Sister, we'll make ourselves very comfy here. Oh, what about church?'

'Of course you're Catholics. Well, if you had transport then the parish church is in town but until then – our own chapel is always open and we have Mass there every morning at seven o'clock. Either Father Malone or Father Stephen offers it. You can walk round by the walls and enter the chapel without needing to go through the grounds. You'll be very welcome.'

It wasn't true, she thought, turning to take her leave. She didn't want these people here in the building Sister Hilaria loved so much. She didn't, if she were to be honest with herself, want them anywhere near the convent at all.

Walking back sombrely she chided herself for judging by appearances and for selfishly wanting to shut out the rest of the world.

'Not having special friendships enables us to be friendly to everybody,' her own novice mistress had instructed. 'Detachment spares us from having to choose our friends on the basis of whether we are drawn to them personally or not. It shields us from selfishness.'

'Did they arrive all right?' Sister Dorothy was passing through the hall and paused to enquire.

'Yes. There are four of them. A friend of the family came to help them settle in.'

'As long as they're not subletting. Oh, Mother David was telling me about your illustrating the book or books for the children – it's a task you'll enjoy doing.'

'They're booklets actually but they may be bound into four or five volumes,' Sister Joan said. 'My sketching won't interfere with your work in the library?'

'Not at all. You'll be using one of the storerooms anyway.'

She smiled and moved off. There was something friendlier and more relaxed in her attitude, Sister Joan thought. Probably she was starting to appreciate the burden of responsibility being rested on other shoulders.

'Is there any more word about Mrs Pearson?' Mother David asked when she went in to report the arrival of Mrs Roye and the Lurgans.

Sister Joan shook her head.

'Oh, Inspector Mill asked if it would be possible for me to help go through her belongings once the coroner has decided it's all right,' she remembered. 'She had no family and no close friends apparently and as she was a Catholic—'

'Though not it seems a fully practising one,' Mother David said. 'Father Malone knew her slightly but she wasn't among his regular communicants. He is having a requiem for her.'

'On Sunday?'

'On Wednesday. That's when the funeral will be. If you are going to help sort her things then you could combine the two activities in one fell swoop.'

'Yes, Mother.'

'And don't forget that on Wednesday evening Father Stephen is hearing our confessions. He's offered to come over since Father Malone will be conducting the funeral.'

'Yes, Mother David.'

'And one other thing, Sister.' The pale eyes twinkled slightly behind the round spectacles. 'Do try not to hold up the rest of us while we wait for you to finish your confession.'

'No, Mother Prioress.'

Mother David, she thought as she quitted the parlour, had a jokey way of reminding her that her list of faults to be forgiven was generally a long one!

She would take the repaired documents back to Father Malone on Wednesday too, she decided. The bleach had worked, eradicating the obscene little drawings and leaving a slight roughness only on the surface of the thick paper. It would be noticed by an expert but since Rome was hardly likely to demand submission of the documents to its archives the danger was very slight indeed.

Nevertheless her mind remained preoccupied during the period of religious studies – today a talk on the meaning of Advent – thoughts crowding in and scurrying around like ants that it was no surprise even to herself when in answer to a question from Mother David about the relevance of Advent in the modern church she replied absently, 'Guy Fawkes.'

'Guy Fawkes Night is hardly a Catholic feast, Sister,' Sister Perpetua observed.

'Because he and his fellow conspirators failed to blow up the Houses of Parliament? Perhaps we ought to celebrate the attempt,' Sister Marie began.

'Oh please, no!' Sister Mary Concepta's gentle voice had risen slightly. 'Please let us not—'

'Sister Mary Concepta is quite right,' Sister Gabrielle said. 'It was a most unfortunate affair, best forgotten.'

Sister Katherine enquired if they were going to have an Advent Calendar.

'With teddy bears and rabbits on I suppose? Honestly, Sister!' Sister Gabrielle said with a snort.

Mother David, glancing at her watch, said brightly that she felt they had covered the subject sufficiently for one day.

'As you have probably heard, the tenants for the old postulancy have arrived. I propose to go over tomorrow morning and welcome them,' she said. 'Sister Hilaria will accompany me. I wish to make it clear that we are, of course, pleased to have them here but that our lives must remain very separate. And, of course, they must feel comfortable about using the chapel since they have no transport. I think that's all. Oh, one more thing. In our prayers let us not forget Mrs Pearson, the elderly lady who died of a heart attack. She apparently has no close relatives or close friends for that matter so we must pray for her with special fervour.'

They made their way out, Sister Gabrielle whispering loudly that if anyone talked nonsense about Guy Fawkes again then she wouldn't be responsible.

'Actually,' Sister Marie murmured to Sister Joan, 'I had a bit of a crush on him when I was in my early teens. All that Spanish glamour and courage – you know.'

'Guy Fawkes was a Yorkshireman in his early forties,' Sister Joan said, amused.

'Oh well!' Sister Marie shrugged cheerfully. 'Lucky we never met! It would have been such a disappointment!'

There was half an hour before supper, Sister Joan thought. She could carry on with a few roughly sketched ideas for the illustrations.

'Sister, there were some carrots in the van. Could I get them?' Sister Marie was asking as they went into the kitchen. 'I thought I'd grate one or two into the vegetable hotpot—'

'The van!' Sister Joan grimaced. 'I left it outside the old postulancy and walked back without thinking! I'd better get it. In ten minutes you shall have your carrots!'

She snatched her cloak from the peg, shut the door firmly against Alice who might delay her by hunting for rabbits, and walked rapidly through the already darkening gardens and past the shrubberies to where the stone steps led down to the abandoned tennis court.

There were lights on in the downstairs window on the right. The curtains had been partly drawn but, as she moved closer, she could see through the wide gap that they were seated at the dining-table, clearly beginning their supper. Mrs Roye, head partly turned away, had taken the largest chair, excusable when one considered her bulk. The thin, pale son-in-law was pouring out the tea.

And if they weren't allowed to make use of the enclosure then she, by the same token, hadn't the slightest right to watch them while they believed themselves to be unobserved.

She turned aside and went through the side gate to where the van had been parked. The back had been secured but the driving seat door was ajar, the ignition key still in place.

She climbed up, checked the bag of carrots was under the front seat where she'd tucked it, and backed out carefully along the outer walls.

The sun had set almost completely, leaving a red rim of farewell below a lowering sky.

A head appeared suddenly above the enclosure wall as she glanced to her left. Instinctively she braked, was blinded suddenly by the glare of a powerful torch and closed her eyes, hearing the wheels of the vehicle screech and stop.

When she opened her eyes again the dazzle of the light remained on their retinas, causing her to blink rapidly. The only glimpse she obtained of the climbing figure was of a black cloak, flung across a face and head she had no chance to distinguish clearly.

The torchlight flashed again and when she opened her

eyes fully the track that curved round the perimeter of the enclosure was empty save for a few straggling bushes at the side.

NINE

'This is splendid, Sister!' Father Malone beamed as he peered at the thin sheaf of documents.

'Mother David thought you would like to have them,' Sister Joan said.

'Yes indeed, and I shall take care to lock them away most securely this time,' he assured her, stooping to the drawer. 'I had not spoken of their loss to Father Stephen or Sister Jerome.'

'I see no need,' she said, giving him, as he paused, the answer he obviously wanted. 'They can have had nothing to do with it and, you know, Father, it is possible that you forgot to lock the drawer in the first place.'

'That's possible,' he admitted. 'I am inclined to be a mite forgetful these days. And this afternoon Mrs Pearson, God rest her soul, is to be buried.'

'Did you know her well, Father?'

'I'm sorry to say hardly at all,' he answered. 'She was a Catholic of course though not a regular communicant. Her husband was not of the Faith, but a good steady man for all that. Jim Pearson. Yes, a nice man. After his death she very seldom came to church but she liked to keep the old church-yard neat and free of litter. Some people get comfort from such things. Will you be coming to the funeral?'

'If I get away in time. I'm deputed to help clear her things.'

'Ah, now she'd've liked that,' he said. 'I mean, having a nun do the job is much better than having some inquisitive member of the public ferreting around. Perhaps I'll see you later then, Sister? God bless!'

She left him carefully and deliberately locking the drawer and got back into the van.

To her pleasure, Inspector Mill was standing at the gate, having evidently just locked his car.

'Good morning, Sister. No religious studies today?' he queried.

'Good morning, and sarcasm is wasted on me,' she retorted equably. 'I'm surprised to see you here though. Surely the forensic people—?'

'Perfectly natural death,' he said.

'But the candles?'

'Nothing in the law says people can't burn peculiar candles. Sergeant Petrie's inside making a rough inventory. So far he hasn't come across a will.'

'A will! Would she have had anything to leave?' she asked, stepping past him towards the open front door.

'The cottage was hers,' he said. 'That might fetch a decent sum these days. She lived on her State Pension and had five hundred pounds in savings. If there are any heirs then—'

'She told me she had no relatives living.'

'Well, you never know – a second cousin or someone might turn up if she died intestate. Petrie, anything up there?'

'Not really, sir.' Sergeant Petrie's solid frame blocked the head of the stairs. 'A big silver fob watch – probably belonged to her husband I should think, a few utilities bills all neatly clipped together, some old photographs in an album – childhood snaps I think – a couple of newspapers with plants pressed inside them.'

'What sorts of plants?' Sister Joan asked.

'Witch hazel, bay, some roses and dahlias – pretty dried up by now – oh, and I had a look in the kitchen cupboard, sir, while you were on your way over. She has packets of beeswax, bottles of vegetable dye and enough sconces to light up St Paul's!'

'And there are the books,' Sister Joan indicated them.

'Catherine Cookson, Daphne du Maurier, Israel Regardie and Dennis Wheatley,' Inspector Mill commented, 'What you might call a Catholic taste.'

'I had a word with one of the neighbours,' Sergeant Petrie said coming down the stairs. 'Mrs Trent. Her lad is working on the boats up-river.'

'What does she have to say?'

'That the old girl – Mrs Pearson, that is – was a bit peculiar. Harmless enough but kept herself to herself, spent a lot of time tidying up the old graveyard, never wanted to stop and chat. Friendly enough but odd. Always talking to her cat.'

'Which in the seventeenth century might've got her arrested and swum as a witch,' Inspector Mill mused. 'I wonder how many innocent old women ended up on the gallows because they cherished a pet animal and didn't mingle with the crowd?'

'Hundreds I daresay,' Sister Joan said with a shiver.

'Right!' Inspector Mill looked round the room. 'I suggest we make a general inventory and parcel up anything that might be of value, put a seal on the doors and windows and leave the rest to the lawyers.'

'I'm not sure what possible use I can be here,' Sister Joan said.

'I thought your eagle eye might've lighted on something,' he said with a teasing look.

'Nothing.'

'In any case we prefer a woman to delve into a woman's things. More fitting somehow,' Sergeant Petrie added.

'And Constable Seldon is manning the station all morning?'

'She's not in today,' Inspector Mill said.

'Oh?'

'Not the politest of recruits.' He looked slightly annoyed. 'No telephone call, just a note lying on my desk when I got in this morning. "Sorry. Family problem. Will contact you." Anyway she clearly isn't ill since she delivered the note by hand. Constable Boswell saw her going into the station. He was checking the duty roster in the outer office. I gave her a ring but her mobile's switched off.'

'Where shall I start?'

'The bedroom – yes, I know, Petrie, you've itemized everything but it won't hurt for someone to have a second look.'

'Point taken, sir!' Petrie said.

Going into the front bedroom again gave Sister Joan a moment of unease. She could see again that staring figure on the bed, the candles burning, almost smell the sweetish, acrid smell as the smoke curled up lazily into the air.

Imagination was a false counseller! The bed had been stripped, the wardrobe door with its few hanging garments and the spare candles and sconces was open, the two drawers of the low dressing-table partly pulled out. Everything was clean and everything had that faintly shabby air that denotes modest means. It was a double bed with two pillows at each side.

The late lamented Jim Pearson must've slept here next to his wife during the years of their happy but childless marriage. No doubt Mrs Pearson had still kept to her side of the bed long after its other occupant was ashes. Had she in her last extremity reached out a hand unavailingly for comfort and found only empty space?

She turned abruptly to pull the drawers out further. There were neatly folded knickers, two bras, a pile of clean white handkerchiefs, a couple of cotton slips, an old style suspender belt and several pairs of stockings – the faint perfume of the rose-patterned lining paper came to her nostrils.

The lower drawer held three sweaters, brightly coloured and obviously hand-knitted. Mrs Pearson would have felt cheered as she sat downstairs, her needles clicking in the somewhat garish colours of the wool.

There were no books here except for the small, dog-eared

album on the bedside table. Picking it up she leafed through it, seeing again the young trim Mrs Pearson in her flowered dresses with other, obvious members of the family. A studio photograph of a fair-haired little girl laughing at something behind the camera was entitled:

My darling Glenda, aged four

And nobody had known that darling Glenda would end up alone, regarded half seriously as the local witch, eyes fixed on some horror with the candles burning around her—

'Inspector Mill! Sergeant Petrie!'

'What is it?'

It was Sergeant Petrie who asked the question, Alan Mill who reached the bedroom first.

'I know why she lit the candles,' Sister Joan said.

'Why?' Inspector Mill asked.

'For protection against whatever she thought she'd seen in the churchyard,' Sister Joan said. 'She was steeped in superstition – hobgoblins, wicked fairies, ghouls – perhaps it amused her in the beginning but things like that, when dwelt upon, can fire the subconscious. She saw someone in the churchyard – some local idiot out to scare her perhaps – nobody believed she had actually seen anything. But she feared it, feared it more because her cat had disappeared! She sensed that real evil was coming near. That was why she got a lift up to the old postulancy and lit all the candles there. To keep evil away! And then she came back here and – something must have happened – something to terrify her – she lit candles in her bedroom to keep the evil out.'

'Devil's piss? Begging your pardon, Sister.' Sergeant Petrie looked unconvinced.

' "The devil hateth a mocking spirit",' she said. 'Putting the asafoetida in the beeswax, and the garlic too – that was mocking him in a way, don't you see? She lit the candles and then she felt safe so she put on her dressing-gown and lay on the bed. She probably felt a bit weak and breathless by then – she'd done a lot of walking the previous evening but at least she was safe. Except that she – wasn't.'

'The Devil came in, did he?' Inspector Mill said.

'I think someone came in, wearing gloves, sliding through the open window in the pantry, came up the stairs – she was frightened to death.'

'It's still not murder,' Inspector Mill said.

'Manslaughter then. At the very least breaking and entering?'

'If that's what actually happened you'd never get a jury to convict anyone of anything without a lot more proof.'

'And there isn't any.'

'Only your fingerprints, Sister, and it's highly unlikely that you dressed up as the Devil and landed in her bedroom.'

'Well, of course I didn't!' she said indignantly.

'Any sign of a will?' Sergeant Petrie asked.

'Not so far. Perhaps she didn't make one.'

She looked at the flat top of the dressing-table on which the silver fob watch, the usual accoutrements of brush, comb and cologne were laid on a lace doily.

'Was that watch there when you found her?' Inspector Mill asked.

'I've no idea. I only saw her. Why?'

'The watch was on the dressing-table when we got here,' Sergeant Petrie said. 'If it was thieves who broke in they'd surely have taken it. That's high grade silver that is. Old, too.'

'No prints?' Inspector Mill looked at him.

'Nothing, sir. There were Mrs Pearson's prints everywhere but that was to be expected.'

'There's an inscription on the back.' Inspector Mill took up the heavy timepiece and read the inscribed word 'James Pearson, a dear grandson.'

'He kept it in memory,' Sister Joan said softly. 'I don't suppose he ever wore it, but it was a link with his childhood.'

'It opens at the back,' Inspector Mill said, without expression. 'Wait a moment. Yes!'

He had extracted a tightly folded and small piece of paper.

'What is it?' Sister Joan asked.

'What I hoped it might be.' He was unfolding the paper very gingerly.

'A will?'

'Short and sweet. "I, Glenda Pearson, leave all I have to the Cats' Protection League." Signed and dated two years ago.'

'No witnesses?' Sergeant Petrie asked.

'Two. Lord, but she couldn't've found thinner paper if she'd tried! A Mr and Mrs Bowles. That must be the couple over on the housing estate who take in stray animals. I'll get this to the local solicitor at once.'

'So there really were no relatives at all.' Sister Joan felt rather sad.

'It seems not, but families can die out over two or three generations. Look at the Tarquins. Well, the Cats' Protection League will be happy about this anyway.'

He folded the paper up very carefully and slipped it into a small plastic folder.

'We'll test it for her prints just to be absolutely sure,' he said, 'but it looks perfectly genuine to me.'

'But why not go to a solicitor?' she queried.

'Solicitors cost money. She was hanging on to her bit of cash. Shall we take a look in the other bedroom and the bathroom now?'

The smaller bedroom overlooked the yard and the quay beyond. It contained a single bed, made up but obviously not slept in and an empty chest of drawers. On a small bedside table was a glass jug and tumbler and an empty biscuit tin.

'The guest who never came,' Sister Joan said.

'Looks like it.' Inspector Mill spoke soberly.

The bathroom was clean and tidy and contained only toothbrush and a mint flavoured toothpaste, a box of tissues and a box filled with an assortment of lipsticks and foundation creams and a bottle of shampoo. In a linen closet let into the wall, clean sheets and towels and an eiderdown cover were neatly piled.

'Not much in the way of occult secrets here!' Inspector Mill commented.

'She was a white witch if she was any sort of witch at all,' Sister Joan said.

'You really believe in that stuff?'

'I believe that good and evil are worked through human agency,' she said soberly. 'Mrs Pearson felt evil coming and tried to do something about it by herself. I wish she had gone to Father Malone.'

'Looks as if there's nothing more to find,' Sergeant Petrie said.

'Almost time for lunch. Will you have some with us, Sister? It's all right! I already rang the convent. Mother David gave permission and she'll see you at the funeral.'

'She's coming herself,' Sister Joan confirmed. 'I think she feels that Mrs Pearson will otherwise be short of mourners.'

'And having a couple of Sisters there will quash any rumours about Mrs Pearson's having spent her spare time riding on a broomstick. Sergeant Petrie and I were thinking of going to the local pub. . . .'

'Suits me fine,' Sister Joan said. 'I can have toasted cheese sandwich and a cup of coffee.'

They went out together, Sergeant Petrie having carefully checked the doors and windows and secured them.

'What about any food in the cupboards?' she asked as they went down the path.

'Mainly tins of cat food and several pints of milk,' Sergeant Petrie told her. 'We thought the Anchor might suit for a bite to eat. No need to drive there.'

'Fine.' She nodded amiably.

The Anchor fronted the quay and was one of the few public houses that had no jukebox and no one-armed bandit. Its furniture was oak and the horse brasses on the walls genuine. It was also the kind of place, well mannered and low key, where nobody was likely to make any salacious comment about a nun with two policemen.

'Did your tenants arrive all right?' Inspector Mill asked.

'I met them at the station after I gave Constable Seldon my fingerprints.'

'Which will of course be destroyed,' Sergeant Petrie assured her.

'It doesn't matter if you don't,' she said with a grin, 'since I wasn't thinking of embarking on a life of crime!'

'If you ever did, Sister,' the Inspector told her, 'I'd back you to get away with it every time.'

'I hope I never feel tempted to put you to the test,' she said with an answering smile before growing serious again. 'Finding the will won't mean the end of the investigation into Mrs Pearson's death, will it?'

'We can't investigate a natural death,' he objected.

'There was a break-in.'

'We've no evidence that anyone broke in except you,' he pointed out. 'Nothing stolen, nothing vandalized, no marks of violence – she died of a heart attack.'

'Malkin didn't!' she interrupted indignantly. 'He was drowned.'

'That's still on file, but I'm afraid you'll find, if anyone ever finds out anything, that was sheer nastiness, Sister! Same with whoever lured Alice away, if anyone did—'

'Or poisoned the lurcher,' Sergeant Petrie put in.

'And we've no proof that the incidents were connected.'

'The dreadful sketches in the book from the postulancy—?'

'Which you yourself put in the refuse bin,' Inspector Mill reminded her.

'You're right.'

'You sound disappointed,' he teased. 'Does a nice juicy murder liven up the religious life then?'

'No, Alan, it doesn't!' Her face flushed with indignation. 'But when a crime does occur then I like to see it solved and someone brought to justice. It's like weeds growing in a garden. A few small ones don't even show but if they're not rooted out they'll spoil the whole garden.'

'We've informed the various societies about the cat and the lurcher and the two fledgings that were killed,' he said. 'They deal with hundreds of worse cases every year. It isn't a pretty little universe.'

'I know,' she conceded. 'I just feel so frustrated at not being able to do anything. Oh, help, is that the time?'

'We'd better make tracks for the funeral,' he agreed.

'Mother David told me at breakfast that she was coming with Sister Hilaria. Father Malone was picking them up in his car. I'd better get back to the van! Inspector, I hope you don't feel that I've been wasting your time with all this.'

'You haven't,' he said, giving her his warmest smile. 'Any suspicious circumstance has to be reported and there are definite signs of vandalism around, so we'll be keeping our eyes open.'

'Thank you – oh, what do I owe—?'

'This is on us – or rather the taxpayer,' Sergeant Petrie assured her. 'Well see you soon, Sister.'

'If you're sure.'

She went out into the still October air.

She had said nothing of the figure she had glimpsed the previous evening. It had been only a momentary flash of a head, a dark cape, and then the light of a powerful torch had blinded her. In any case the suggestion, which he had clearly made in fun, that she enjoyed the challenge of a murder investigation had stung a little.

She drove sedately to the church, parked neatly and was in time to slide into the pew next to Sister Hilaria before the organ sounded its first sombre note and the coffin, with a single wreath of golden dahlias on it was borne up the aisle by four men from the regular congregation.

Requiems, she thought, were always sad affairs but they could be rendered more tolerable by anecdotes about the departed, by friends talking over old times. This afternoon there was indeed a number of people in the church but she suspected that the presence of the police at the cottage had brought several of them out of curiosity.

The Twenty-Third Psalm and the interdenominational 'All Things Bright and Beautiful' were sung by the thinly scattered congregation and the coffin was borne out on the shoulders of its bearers.

'Mrs Pearson told Father several years ago that she wished to be cremated,' Mother David said quietly to Sister Joan as they came out of the building. 'Apparently she wished her ashes to be mingled with those of her late husband's. Sister Hilaria and I will attend the short service at the Crrematorium and then Father Malone has kindly invited us to take tea with him before he gives us a lift home. You didn't find anything?'

'The police are convinced it was a natural death, Mother Prioress.'

'Then that is something to be grateful for. We will see you later, Sister.'

'Yes, Mother.'

Going along the path she glanced back and saw that Inspector Mill and Sergeant Petrie had joined the other two nuns and were talking quietly.

Ought she to mention the cloaked figure of the previous evening? No, probably not. The incident was too nebulous to describe clearly and she hadn't a shade of evidence.

Like Mrs Pearson, she thought suddenly. The old lady had spoken of a figure capering by a grave, had seen silver horns – a mask of some kind obviously. She hadn't mentioned a cape.

It would do no harm, she thought, climbing up into the van, to have a quick look around the enclosure walls before she continued on into the convent proper.

When she reached the moor she was startled by a loud honking as a car overtook her, driving so fast that she was forced on to the rough grass.

'Hey, be careful!'

Impossible to display the patience of a saint when there were dangerous drivers around.

To her surprise, the car, a neat saloon, pulled up just ahead of her with a squeal of brakes and a young girl emerged, striding back towards the van. Her slim figure was enhanced by a high-necked black sweater and black drainpipe trousers that clung to impossibly long legs.

'You're a nun!' she said.

'Almost a dead nun,' Sister Joan said scathingly. 'You were driving like a maniac! This really isn't a properly tarmacked—'

'Spare the lecture!' The girl tossed back a thick strand of gleaming red hair. 'Nobody tells me how to drive! I'm looking for a place called the postulancy – my mum is renting it.'

'Your mother being—?'

'Mrs Winifred Roye.'

'And you are—?'

'Kit Roye. Which way is it?'

'If you follow me' – Sister Joan put definite emphasis on the word follow – 'then I happen to be passing it.'

'Cool! And who are you?'

'I'm Sister Joan,' she said.

'Of course, praying Marys don't have surnames, do they?'

'If you're studying bad manners,' Sister Joan said, 'then you ought to pass first grade with flying colours.'

The girl stared at her for a moment, then laughed.

'Hey! you've a neat tongue!' she said. 'I'll follow you then. This is a back of beyond kind of place, isn't it?'

'Back of beyond is what we happen to like,' Sister Joan said. 'I wasn't aware there were any more of you.'

'Ah! you've met Henry, the eternal guest and hanger-on!' The girl laughed again. 'I'm only here for a couple of weeks. I've brought the car since they don't have transport.'

And thank the Lord for that, Sister Joan thought uncharitably, because now we won't have them cluttering up our chapel.

It was such an ungracious thought that she said a hasty *mea culpa* and then audibly invited the newcomer to follow her.

It was no more than ten minutes before they reached the gate. Sister Joan drew up and indicated the building beyond.

'They'll still be sorting things out, I daresay,' she said, putting her head out of the van window.

'Thanks!'

Kit Roye, drawing up behind her, honked the horn loudly again.

'Kit, pet! Is that you?'

The overblown figure waddled to the gate, scarf tied round head, mop in hand.

'No, Mum, it's Lady Godiva!' Kit said, jumping out of the car and rushing to embrace her parent. 'I've brought the car. Neat, isn't she?'

'Bit small. Not much leg room,' Mrs Roye said, emerging to nod briefly to Sister Joan and examine the vehicle. 'Won't fit us all.'

'It will if Ian runs behind,' Kit said brightly.

'Now don't you start on Ian!' Mrs Roye began.

'Start on him? I wouldn't even finish him for pudding!' Kit cried.

The two of them hugged again, their laughter splintering the peace of the afternoon.

'Is there anything we can do for you, Sister?' Mrs Roye enquired, breaking away from her daughter.

'No, no, thank you,' Sister Joan said hastily. 'Good afternoon.'

Driving on, she decided any examination of the place where she had seen the cloaked figure would have to wait until there were no witnesses.

TEN

'How are the drawings coming on, Sister?' Sister Dorothy, making an inventory of library books, looked up as Sister Joan came from the storeroom.

'Not too badly, thank you, Sister. I've reached St David but he's proving a bit of a problem,' she confessed. 'I know he's patron of Wales, but real information about him does seem to be a bit scanty save that he was a rabid teetotaller and that is hardly likely to excite eight-year-old kids.'

'His mother,' Sister Dorothy said helpfully, 'was St Non. She was a nun but whether before or after his birth the records don't tell.'

'Oh dear!'

The two of them stared at each other for a moment and then unexpectedly Sister Dorothy laughed.

'Very few are born natural saints,' she said. 'Some of them led high old lives before the Holy Spirit descended!'

'I don't think Mother David will be dwelling on the former aspect,' Sister Joan said, with an answering chuckle. 'Do go and look at them if you have time. Criticism is always welcome.'

'Oh no it isn't.'

Sister Dorothy smiled again. Being one of the sisters instead of prioress had brought out her human side, Sister Joan thought, as she went down the spiral stairs into the chapel.

Genuflecting to the altar, she reflected that life had settled over the last couple of days into its usual peaceful pattern. She had found an opportunity to go over and look along the enclosure wall but there was no trace of anything, no broken coping or dislodged stone to suggest that anyone had climbed over it recently.

'Sister Joan, are you busy?'

Mother David emerged from the parlour.

'Not particularly, Mother. What can I do—?'

'There's been a telephone call from the Mothers' Union. The chairwoman has a surplus of gifts donated for the parish party on October the tenth – or is it ninth? – at all events she'd be grateful if someone could go down and pick out anything that might be useful for the Children's Home.'

'She can't do it herself?'

'Apparently there was a slight contretemps several weeks ago between the respective chairwomen,' Sister David said, twitching her nose in token of amusement. 'One ought not to pander to such idiocy but a gift from one lot to the other might pave the way to harmony.'

'And you think I can act as ministering angel.'

'Oh no,' Mother David said in faint surprise. 'You happen to be the only one who drives the van!'

'I'll go at once,' Sister Joan said, suiting action to words. The damp drizzling of the rain that had never quite settled had dried into crispness. She put on her cloak, went out and started up the engine.

Alice, stretched out just within the stable, lifted her head and then, apparently preferring the society of her companion who munched hay contentedly, lay down again.

Automatically Sister Joan slowed as she passed the old postulancy, but the curtains in the lower windows were drawn close though the glow of firelight shone through. The car was parked neatly outside.

At least the family kept within their prescribed limits, she mused, and chided herself mentally for being ungracious. The rent they paid was helping the Order and their somewhat rough manners might be softened by their proximity to the convent.

She called at the church and picked up a quantity of clothes and toys which would certainly be put to good use in the Children's Home.

By the time she had delivered them and agreed that the chairwoman of the Mothers' Union was, at heart, a delightful woman, the hands of her fob watch were creeping round to three. Still an hour and a half before religious studies, time to work out how to portray St David, but for the moment sketching had lost its charms.

She parked the van and took herself for a brisk walk along the main street. This being Friday some goods in the shops were being reduced. Sister Marie had mentioned they were getting low on coffee—

'Sister Joan, good afternoon!'

'Sergeant Petrie, nice to see you.'

She shook hands cheerfully, noticing as she did so that his own usual smile seemed somewhat forced.

'On your errands as usual?' he enquired.

'I do do other tasks occasionally,' she protested. 'Are you—?'

'Run off our feet as ever!'

'Not more vandalism, I hope?'

'Nothing to write home about. No, Constable Boswell has a bout of the flu and Constable Seldon hasn't turned up yet.'

'But she said family problems, didn't she, in the note she left?'

'She did indeed, and when she didn't turn up this morning the inspector had me try her mobile again. Still switched off. So he dug out her home address, not wanting to alarm them but a mite miffed you could say.'

'And?'

'He made some excuse about checking up on something and her mother said she was still down here. Hadn't gone home at all. Well, Inspector Mill made some kind of excuse, thought she'd had a couple of days coming to her, and rang off. I'm on my way to her digs to see what's up.'

'Where does she lodge?'

'Up in Beldon Street. Got a bedsit over the antique shop. I don't suppose you've time . . .'

He looked at her hopefully.

'I can walk up with you if you like,' she offered.

'I'd be grateful,' he said promptly. 'That shop only opens three days a week – too expensive for regular trading. Mr Laurence – he owns the place – lives up near the hospital. Says he saw her on Tuesday coming in from duty but she went out again directly. Anyway he gave me the keys so I could have a look round.'

'She might've been taken ill,' Sister Joan said, matching her stride to his.

The shop with its barred shutters discouraging thieves stood at the end of the street. At its other side an arched entrance led through to the back. Sergeant Petrie inserted his key in the lock and ushered her through a darkened room, where various objects glinted, towards a staircase.

'The bedsit's up top,' he said. 'There's a locked door. Old Mr Laurence used to live there himself but his rheumatics were getting a mite troublesome so he went to live with his daughter and rented the top floor out. Seemed like good sense, he said, to have a policewoman on the premises.'

He went ahead of her, switching on the light at the top of the dim stairs and carefully unlocking the door.

'Still got the shutters closed,' he observed, going into the darkened space. 'Constable Seldon?'

His voice echoed queerly through the space.

'There's a switch here.' Sister Joan pressed it and a row of small lamps sprang into life along one wall.

'Nice,' Sergeant Petrie said appreciatively. 'Very nice.'

What had been one large apartment had been converted into an open-plan living cum sleeping area with a tiled section denoting kitchen and bathroom separated from the living area by a half wall. A curtain, drawn back and secured to a large hook, displayed the sleeping area at the far end. A single bed was neatly made and a half open wardrobe door revealed several skirts and sweaters hanging on the rail.

'Well, she's not here,' Sergeant Petrie announced unnecessarily.

'Not even a cup draining in the sink. She must be very tidy,' Sister Joan said, switching on another light.

'Her uniform's not here,' he said, looking at the clothes.

'Was she wearing uniform when she left the note in Inspector Mill's office on Monday morning?'

'No reason to if she wasn't coming in on duty. I'll check with Constable Boswell anyway.'

'And if she'd been carrying a suitcase he'd have noticed that?'

'I never thought to ask him,' Sergeant Petrie said. 'He might have done but he was busy – anyway she could have left it just inside the main door while she popped into the office.'

'The clothes hangers on the rail are all filled except for one,' Sister Joan pointed out.

'And there are two suitcases under the bed.' He had bent to look and now pulled them out.

'Anything in them?' she asked.

'A few newspaper clippings.'

'About what?'

'See for yourself!' He handed her the neatly cut and clipped pieces of newspaper. 'I'd better get on to the station.'

He moved away leaving her to leaf through the clippings.

They were old ones, at least three years old, though the dates above the headings were badly smudged.

FOURTEEN-YEAR-OLD BOY SUICIDES IN LOCAL WOOD, one heading ran.

Sister Joan moved closer to the light and read on.

A tragic discovery yesterday morning revealed the body of Simon Bartlett, the fourteen-year-old boy whose disappearance was first reported a week ago. Simon, a

129

pupil at the Westcliff High School, had been unusually silent and depressed in recent weeks according to his teacher, Grace Swan. She had asked him what was troubling him but received no reply. An inquest will be held but police are already convinced that no other person was involved. Meddlers' Wood, once a well-known beauty spot popular with picnic parties was recently scheduled for development due to the diseased state of several trees. It had also become well known for the drug takers who went there. The police have stated that Simon Bartlett had no known connection with anything of that nature.

Another clipping showed a grainy photograph of a young lad with an open smiling countenance and a cowlick of light hair over his forehead. The eyes, she thought, were well spaced, the mouth irresolute.

She was looking at the third – a brief account of the shortage of uniformed police in parts of Cornwall when Sergeant Petrie finished his call and moved back to stand beside her.

'Inspector Mill's on his way over, Can you wait until he arrives?'

'Yes, but I can't wait long.' She passed him the clippings.

'Can't say I recall this,' he said. 'Not on our patch. Looks like a nice kid. Mind, at that age they can take it into their heads to do some odd things!'

'He came from Constable Seldon's home town.'

'Maybe she knew him or his family.'

'And kept the clippings for – three years? There are no other newspaper clippings anywhere.'

'She'd've been just about starting her police training then,' he observed. 'Went to the Police College. Modern methods, paperwork, all that kind of thing – not to mention computers! Can't stand the things myself. It's worrying though when a perfectly good colleague goes missing.'

'She was stationed at Plymouth then after her training.

When did she apply to transfer here?'

'No more than five or six weeks back,' Sergeant Petrie said. 'Inspector Mill took her on like a shot. This may be a small place but it still needs decent policing.'

'Nothing in here.' Sister Joan had moved to a small chest of drawers and slid out the top one.

'Nothing?'

'Some make-up and handkerchiefs, comb and a brush. And underwear in the drawer below. No letters or papers I mean.'

'Very neat,' Sergeant Petrie approved.

'No personal photographs, no letters, no cards?'

'Making a fresh start?' he suggested. 'That sounds like the inspector now. I'll go down and let him in.'

He went down the carpeted staircase.

Making a fresh start after what? Sister Joan wondered. Why would a young woman join the Force, work steadily for three years and then get herself transferred to a little Cornish back-water? Inspector Mill and Petrie and Constable Boswell had family here, local connections, ties.

'How are you, Sister Joan?' Alan Mill had entered, nodding to her amiably. 'So what's been going on then in your opinion, Sergeant?'

'I'd've said she'd done a bunk, sir,' Sergeant Petrie said, 'but all her clothes except her uniform are here. Very few personal effects though.'

'These were in one of the suitcases under the bed,' Sister Joan said, handing him the cuttings.

'Only these?'

She nodded.

'I can't say I recall this case but suicide isn't rare among the young these days unfortunately.'

'There must be some connection surely?'

'I'll get on to Plymouth and find out,' he assured her. 'She came to us at somewhat short notice but her references from the Plymouth Force were good. Right, let's lock up and be on our way.'

'Will she be put on the missing persons list?' Sister Joan asked as they went down the stairs.

'Not yet – not officially, but I'll set a few things in motion. It's only been a couple of days and I don't want to get any black marks on her record at this early stage of her career.'

Now was the time to tell him about the cloaked figure perhaps? She opened her mouth to speak when Inspector Mill's mobile rang.

'Yes? Yes. Where? When? Right, on my way.' His normally pleasant voice was suddenly harsh.

'In a moment, Sister.' He delayed her question with a half-lifted hand. 'That was Boswell. Someone just reported a body.'

'Who—?'

'Not formally identified yet of course, but it's a female, blonde hair, early twenties. Wearing a bra and panty girdle, wrapped in a cloak. Fished out of the river about twenty minutes ago. Forensics are on their way.'

'Inspector,' she said quickly, 'this may not be relevant but on Monday evening I went down to collect the van from outside the old postulancy. A cloaked figure was climbing over the wall just ahead of me as I drove it round the outer walls. I had to brake sharply because a torch was shone full in my face dazzling me. When I had gathered my wits the figure had gone.'

'Man or woman?'

'Impossible to tell. I half convinced myself that I'd imagined it.'

'Probably unrelated,' he said. 'We'd best get off. Thank you, Sister. If we need extra help you'll be able to come?'

'Provided Mother David agrees, but I don't think I can be of help this time.'

She nodded to them and went on into the main street.

In the parlour, Mother David looked anxious and alarmed as she finished her recital of events.

'This is most unsettling news, Sister,' she said, eyes blinking rapidly behind their lenses. 'I hope it's not the young policewoman, but if not then it must be some other poor soul, may she rest in peace. You should have told me about the cloaked figure you saw.'

'I began to think that I'd imagined it,' Sister Joan said.

'Well, there is nothing we can do except pray,' Mother David said. 'I have always believed that prayer should be our first recourse and not our last. There is no point in saying anything to the other sisters since it doesn't concern us directly. Will you tell the rest that religious studies will be delayed for half an hour? I have a telephone call to make.'

Sister Marie, informed of the delay, looked pleased.

'I needed to look up something on St Martha,' she said. 'She was the one always worrying about the housework so I'm finding out what I can about her.'

'Our Lord rebuked her for paying more attention to that than to His words,' Sister Joan reminded her.

'Typical of a man!' Sister Gabrielle, stumping in from the infirmary, snorted as she spoke.

'Sister, it was Our Blessed Lord who—' Sister Marie began.

'Even so! I promise you, Sister, you can rake the Holy Gospels from end to end and you'll not find Him or any of the disciples helping to dry the dishes,' Sister Gabrielle said.

She helped herself to a stray biscuit and went out.

'She says some very – unexpected things,' Sister Marie said.

'She's getting on.' Sister Joan excused.

It occurred to her as she turned back to the sink where she was rinsing some cups that she had never in her life heard Sister Gabrielle utter a single kindly word about any member of the male population. Some long ago souring experience? There were often many reasons for entering the religious life and not all of them were confided to the novice mistress.

The rest of the day passed without incident. Nothing was said about the most recent discovery. During the last prayers before the grand silence she found her mind wandering away from petitions for more patience and less craving for excitement to hoping that the body had been a complete stranger, someone swept down-river from further up the coast. Not that that itself wasn't sad enough but though she had hardly taken to the new police officer it was deeply disturbing to think of that pert, beautifully made-up face rigid in death, the blonde hair tangled and soaked with salt water.

It was mid morning when the inspector's car nosed up the drive. Sister Joan, having just completed a comic sketch of St George menacing a Disney type dragon was washing her hands in the kitchen when she saw the inspector coming into the yard.

'Mother David said that I'd find you here,' he said, without preamble. 'Good morning, Sister Marie. Can you spare Sister Joan for twenty minutes?'

'Yes, of course, Inspector Mill.' Sister Marie beamed at him cheerfully.

'Did Mother David send you round the back?' Sister Joan asked as they went through to the hall.

'I walked round that way to hail Alice, but she's not around.'

'Off chasing something or other.'

'Well, at least she took no hurt from her adventure. Good morning, Mother David.'

'Good morning again,' she corrected. '*Dominus vobiscum.*'

'*Et cum spiritu,*' Sister Joan said.

Inspector Mill had seated himself on a chair at a little distance.

'You have news for us?' Mother David asked.

'The young woman in the river has been identified as Melanie Seldon, aged twenty-four, our newest member of the local Force,' he said in a formal tone.

'May her soul and the souls of all the faithful departed—' The sisters crossed themselves as the prioress spoke the traditional words.

'Yes, indeed.' He looked faintly embarrassed. 'Of course, the death has no direct link with the convent or any of the sisters but in view of certain recent troubling events – Constable Seldon came to us very recently having transferred from her home town in Plymouth. In her case at the bedsit she rents – rented – were some newspaper clippings. Perhaps you would like to see them?'

He had extracted them from his briefcase and rose to hand them to Mother David who settled her glasses more securely on her small nose and began to read.

'Was there some connection?' she asked at last, looking up.

'Not one we knew about. I've been talking to her father by telephone this morning. Reginald Seldon. Nice man I think. He and his wife were divorced when Melanie, their daughter, was a very small child.'

'Sad,' Mother David said briefly.

'Par for the course these days, Mother David. Not all couples live together happily after ever. Anyway he kept in contact with his daughter at fairly regular intervals. She kept his surname. She apparently got on well with her stepfather who died a couple of years ago. His name was—'

'Bartlett?' Sister Joan could contain herself no longer.

'You're ahead of me as usual, Sister. Yes, the stepfather was Philip Bartlett, and he and the former Mrs Seldon had a child – Simon.'

'The unfortunate boy who—?' Mother David looked distressed.

'He definitely committed suicide,' the inspector said. 'He left a note. I've requested a copy of it. As far as is known he'd got himself mixed up with a pretty fast crowd and was being threatened. But it was suicide while the balance of the mind was disturbed.'

'Of course,' Mother David said. 'Poor child!'

'After the death of her second husband, Mrs Bartlett reverted to her original married name of Seldon.'

'There was a reconciliation?'

'No, Reginald Seldon had remarried. There had been a lot of publicity about Simon Bartlett's death and I suspect she wanted to close that chapter in her life completely.'

'And Melanie joined the Police Service,' Sister Joan said.

'She was apparently devoted to her half brother.' His face was grave. 'We can never be sure now but I would hazard the guess that she had some idea in her mind of bringing those who had driven him to it to justice.'

'But she requested a transfer here,' Sister Joan said.

'Which makes me wonder if she wasn't following some private agenda of her own. She seems to have left no written indications.'

'And now she's dead too.'

'And it definitely was not suicide.' There was distaste in his tone as he continued. 'She didn't drown. Someone hit her on the back of the head hard enough to kill her. Exactly where this happened we don't yet know. Most of the bleeding would have been internal anyway. She was stripped to her underwear whether in her bedsit or elsewhere we also don't know, wrapped in a cloak, a black evening cloak she possessed, and weighed down with stones. It was probably murder.'

'Only probably?' Sister Joan stared at him in astonishment.

'Whoever hit her might not have intended to do more than stun her. When he or she discovered she was dead there may have been panic, an attempt to wash away the traces – who knows? Anyway there it is.'

'She left a note saying there was family trouble on Wednesday morning, so—?'

'The forensic people – I've just come from there – say she has been dead for about five days.'

'Today is Saturday. That means—'

'She was probably killed sometime on Monday, Tuesday at the latest. I don't pretend to understand the science of it but they seem pretty confident.'

'But she went into the station on Wednesday morning to say that—'

Sister Joan broke off as his mobile shrilled.

'Please excuse me, Mother David, Sister.' Rising, he moved to the door, listening, rapping out an occasional word.

'The note left by Simon Bartlett is on its way,' he said,

coming back to his seat. 'There's no doubt he wrote it. Sergeant Petrie just quoted its contents to me.'

'Are we permitted—?' Mother David looked a question.

'Short and obviously emanating from a mind deeply disturbed,' Inspector Mill said. 'It was found in his pocket. "Sorry, sorry. Can't go on. They are legion".'

'My God!' Sister Joan had started up out of her chair. 'Mrs Pearson said that to me when I was leaving her. "They are legion". She said that.'

'Meaning that in contrast to the Oneness of Good, evil is divided and split,' Mother David said.

'Theology was never my particular forte, Mother.' He was rising, his expression still preoccupied. 'Well, there you have it. I wanted to keep you in the picture.'

'And to borrow Sister Joan no doubt?'

Mother David had smiled slightly.

'One hesitates to ask but—'

'Sister Joan has a knack – a most worldly knack – of getting involved in the pursuit of justice,' Mother David said. 'Provided it doesn't interfere with her religious duties then obviously like any member of the public she has my leave to co-operate to the fullest extent. Was there anything else, Inspector?'

'The telephone call interrupted me. If – and it seems quite definite – Melanie Seldon was killed on last Monday or Tuesday then—'

'Who took the note into the station on Wednesday morning?' Sister Joan finished for him.

'Constable Boswell was in the outer office. He saw her going past but they didn't speak. She whisked into my office and left the note and presumably left at once while he was sorting out the duty rota.'

'He saw someone in uniform going into the office,' Sister Joan said. 'Was the note in her handwriting?'

'I brought it with me.' He opened his briefcase again and took out the slip of paper. 'It's like her handwriting certainly, though if it isn't I daresay an expert will spot the difference, and the signature—'

'Has a backward loop,' Sister Joan said, staring at the brief message.

'There were no prints,' he said.

'But she surely wouldn't've written it with gloves on?' Mother David said.

'No, it's not very likely,' he agreed.

'Then it is a forgery?'

'Probably, but there's no way of telling. What you're looking at is a photocopy.'

'With back slanting loops,' Sister Joan said again.

Her voice was unusually subdued.

ELEVEN

'You've heard about the murder, Sister?' Padraic Lee hailed her as she rode Lilith into the camp.

'The woman police officer, yes. It was – shocking.'

The word seemed inadequate but she couldn't think of a more appropriate one.

'Will you look into it?' he enquired.

'I think the police are already looking into it very thoroughly,' she demurred.

'Not that I've any love for the local bobbies, but we can't have someone knocking them off, can we? Cup of tea, Sister?'

'I won't say no.' She dismounted, tethered the pony loosely to a stake as he nipped into the vardo to emerge with two spotlessly clean mugs.

A week had passed. The inquest had been adjourned and the funeral set for the following Monday.

'I'm actually here to pay you for the last lot of fish you brought over,' she said. 'We had them with butter sauce. Sister Marie has herself a job for life, I think!'

'Now you know perfectly well, Sister, that I take no money for any fish that happen to jump in my net when the convent's short,' he said reproachfully. 'You put that away now and don't go offering it again.'

'Sister Marie said you'd say that,' she told him.

'Ah, she's a nice young thing is Sister Marie. How is Sister

139

Teresa though? Now she was a real nice one was Sister Teresa.'

'Caring for her sick father. He has a wasting disease. Of course we hope she will eventually return to us but the Mother House may have other plans for her. Many are needed in the mission field.'

'If you ask me,' Padraic said, 'there's enough wickedness here without going looking for it.'

'I suppose that's a point of view. How are the girls?'

To her surprise his face clouded slightly.

'In school I hope,' he said briefly.

'You hope? Don't you know?'

'Edith's no trouble,' he said, still frowning. 'She's doing well, but Tabitha's getting a mite above herself. Missing classes without leave and hanging round the amusement arcade on Saturdays. I worry about her.'

'Tabitha's fifteen. She's trying her wings.'

'She's trying them too fast for my liking,' he said moodily. 'We Roms have always been respectable – well, bar the odd parcel falling off a lorry or a pheasant for the pot, but we don't let our girls stray. If you see her I'd be glad if you had a word. Now what?'

A sleek car was nosing round the perimeter of the camp where it stopped and an equally sleek figure emerged, carrying a bundle.

'It's Father Stephen!' Sister Joan said in surprise.

'What's he doing here? Doesn't usually stoop this low,' Padraic muttered.

'Good afternoon, Sister Joan. Mr Lee, isn't it?' Father Stephen deposited his bundle on the ground. 'I heard of the loss of your lurcher and it occurred to me . . . my cousin keeps lurchers and one of them had a litter six months back. This young fellow needed a home and it occurred to me that you might find a use for him.'

'You have a cousin who keeps lurchers?' Sister Joan said in surprise.

Somehow she had never considered Father Stephen as being a member of a family.

'I wasn't born wearing the stole, Sister,' he said with unexpected humour. 'If you think you can train the dog then he's yours.'

'He's a fine youngling,' Padraic said, lifting the squirming puppy on to his lap. 'I'm obliged to you, Father. Now there's a piece of luck to brighten the day! I'll call him Kushti, Romany for good luck. And if you ever run out of fish—'

'Oh, the presbytery is kept well supplied,' Father Stephen said, somewhat hastily. 'I must be on my way. Good afternoon to you both.'

He nodded and took his leave, carefully sidestepping a burnt-out fire on the trampled ground nearby.

'He's not such a bad lad after all,' Padraic said.

'No, it appears that he isn't,' Sister Joan said, contritely, as she rearranged some of the opinions she held about the young priest. 'I have to go myself. If I do see Tabitha I'll try to have a word but I can't promise anything.'

'I wouldn't want her disgracing the memory of her late mother,' Padraic said, loyal as ever to the memory of his alcoholic wife.

'I'm certain she won't do that,' Sister Joan said. 'Thanks for the tea.'

He lifted a hand as she untied Lilith and remounted.

There was, she mused, as she trotted back to the convent, a lull in events. For a week she had been able to get on with her conventual life without interruption.

There had been no sign of the tenants for days. Certainly they kept strictly to their own domain. Once she had seen washing on a line at the side of the postulancy and the car still stood there though whether any of the family ever used it to attend the parish church she had no idea.

She drew rein as she reached the gate just in time to avoid colliding with Ian Lurgan who, clad in jeans and a bomber jacket, had just emerged from the side gate.

'Afternoon, Sister,' he said.

'Good afternoon, Mr Lurgan. Settling in?'

'No luck on the job front,' he said, blinking up at her. 'I was wondering if there was anything needed doing up at the convent.'

'Doing?' she queried.

'Odd jobs, bit of painting, electrics – I can turn my hand to most things.'

'Then surely you could find a job locally?'

'Not easy in the winter,' he said. 'People get their houses done up in the summer before the rains start. And they don't take to strangers round here.'

'I don't believe there's anything but I can certainly ask. Do you have references?'

'I could probably dig some out,' he said.

'I'll ask Mother David. I can't go employing you on my own account.'

She gathered up the reins again but he shifted his stance, his hand on the pony's nose.

'It must be rotten being a nun,' he said.

'No, of course it's not!' she said, slightly nettled by what appeared to be sympathy in his tone.

'No freedom?'

'We're all perfectly free. We can walk out any time we like.'

'And no sex. Unless—' He tilted his sandy head at her. 'Is it true that all nuns are lesbians?'

'It certainly is not! Now if you don't mind—'

'I didn't mean to be rude.' He had flushed slightly. 'I just wonder about things from time to time, you see.'

Some people did wonder she supposed, but few ever put the question bluntly.

'You would do better to wonder about other things,' she said aloud. 'As a Catholic—'

'Oh, I'm not a Catholic,' he broke in. 'Dawn and her mum are. I'm nothing in particular. I belong to every religion in a way.'

'How confusing for you,' she said coldly.

142

'But we are married, even if it wasn't in church. I mean God wasn't around.'

'God's always around,' she said firmly. 'Mr Lurgan, I really must get on—'

'And Dawn doesn't really believe in anything,' he went on regardless. 'She wouldn't act the way she does if she did.'

'I don't think—'

'Other men.' He mouthed rather than spoke the words. 'Before we got wed, and afterwards. Women too. It bothers me sometimes.'

'If you have marital problems Father Malone can recommend a good counseller – and there's Relate.'

'Oh, I couldn't talk about it,' he said. 'I hoped after we got wed she might change but she never has. Sorry, Sister, I didn't mean to make you late for anything.'

To her relief he stepped back and she flicked Lilith so sharply on the nose that the latter fairly bounded forward almost unseating her.

'You look hot and bothered,' Sister Marie commented, when she went into the kitchen.

'I gave Lilith her head on the way home,' Sister Joan said.

'Was Padraic Lee pleased with the payment for the fish?'

'Oh, he wouldn't accept the money. Here it is. If you still feel guilty about aiding and abetting a poacher you can put it in the collection box or something. Isn't it nearly time for religious studies?'

'Yes,' Sister Marie said, wisely not commenting on the irritable note in her fellow nun's voice.

'This afternoon,' Mother David said brightly, 'we are going to consider the renewal of our vows which we take every year. Why do we renew them?'

'To remind ourselves they are not just words,' Sister Katherine said.

'Indeed they are not. We vow ourselves to chastity, poverty, obedience and compassion. That last is peculiar to our Order. But shall we start with chastity?'

143

'Cleanliness of mind and body,' Sister Dorothy said.

'But marriage is a sacrament,' Sister Martha objected.

'Chastity is equally valid in marriage as out of it. The only difference is that we have made a spiritual marriage and, just as a husband and a wife must remain loyal and faithful, then so must we. Chastity is not a negative thing.'

'But sometimes,' Sister Marie piped up, 'one cannot avoid seeing someone, say a very handsome man and just wondering for a moment. . . ?'

'Looking at the cover of a book,' Sister Dorothy stated, 'does not entitle us to read it.'

'And poverty?' Sister Gabrielle tapped her stick on the floor.

'I was just coming to that, Sister. Poverty is one of our great strengths. To amass wealth for one's own selfish purpose is to be truly poor.'

'Then God bless the government!' Sister Gabrielle said loudly. 'They certainly help us keep that vow!'

There were stifled giggles.

'Poverty doesn't mean that we must go hungry,' Sister Marie said.

'No indeed not, Sister.' Mother David smiled. 'We are all entitled to sufficient food to keep us healthy, sufficient heat to prevent us from freezing to death, and clothes to preserve our modesty. But the trappings of personal wealth only detract from the joy of knowing that we are not here to lay up treasures on earth.'

'And obedience?' Sister Martha, asking the question, looked eager.

'Obedience to that which is right and sensible,' Sister Dorothy said.

'And who judges that?' Sister Mary Concepta asked gently.

'Obedience to the Rule. Anything contrary to the Rule must be resisted.'

'That's the hard part,' Sister Marie said. 'When the grand silence begins I always remember something I forgot to tell somebody!'

There were sympathetic murmurs of assent.

'If you knit something,' Sister Katherine said timidly, 'and you drop one stitch then the whole garment is ruined.'

'Exactly, Sister!' Mother David looked gratified. 'However we must always use our common sense in such matters. If the house is on fire or someone is taken suddenly ill, then the grand silence may be broken only to the extent that speech is absolutely necessary.'

'Saint Teresa considered that blind obedience showed a lack of intelligence,' Sister Hilaria volunteered.

'Like when a novice came and asked her what to do with a worm she'd found in the garden and Saint Teresa joked she'd better fry it for supper and found the poor novice doing just that,' Sister Gabrielle said with a snort of laughter.

'Exactly! Common sense goes a long way,' Mother David agreed. 'So to compassion. How would you define that, Sister Joan? Sister?'

'I'm sorry, Mother Prioress. What did you say?'

'Concentration helps when we are discussing serious matters,' Mother David said.

'I'm sorry, Mother Prioress.'

'We had reached compassion,' Sister Mary Concepta said helpfully.

'Ruth, pity, sympathy.'

Sister Joan dragged her attention back to the matters under discussion.

'Compassion for a victim is easy,' Sister Dorothy said.

'I sometimes feel that too much compassion for the wrong-doer is shown these days,' Sister Martha ventured.

'Only sometimes?' Sister Gabrielle said. 'I always think that. Whoever poisoned Padraic Lee's dog and murdered that poor young police officer is an out and out criminal and I haven't got an atom of sympathy for them!'

'We don't know for sure that Mr Lee's dog was poisoned deliberately and we certainly don't know it had any connection with the recent tragic event,' Sister Dorothy said.

'Compassion for the sinner,' Sister Hilaria said, 'does not mean condoning the sin.'

'Which sums up the problem nicely. One must try to separate the two,' Mother David agreed. 'Sister Joan, have you anything to contribute to the discussion?'

She looked at her encouragingly.

'I think it's almost impossible to hate the sin and love the sinner,' Sister Joan said bluntly.

'Which is why we are in the religious life,' Sister Hilaria mused. 'We must accomplish the almost impossible. Personally I have always had a certain sympathy for King Herod.'

'Sister, you can't mean that!' Sister Marie exclaimed.

'Not that I condone his actions,' Sister Hilaria allowed, 'but he had a very difficult wife and stepdaughter.'

'So!' Mother David clapped her hands. 'Shall we leave it there for today? The vows we will soon be renewing require private meditation,' she continued. There was still an hour before chapel. Sister Joan, feeling she had somehow let the side down by her inattention, repaired to the stable to give Lilith her rub down and feed.

Smoothing the silky mane it occurred to her that the pony was getting on in years. Lilith had been left over when the convent acquired the Tarquin property and must be elderly by now. When she went there would be small excuse for keeping a horse especially when there was the van in which to get down into town for any necessary business. The thought saddened her. Lilith, like Alice, had become part of the community.

A slight cough behind made her jump slightly.

As she turned, Ian Lurgan, leaning against the stable door, said 'Sorry, Sister Joan. Didn't mean to frighten you!'

'Then you shouldn't creep up on people!' she said sharply.

'I always walk softly, Sister. Very light on my feet.'

'And you're not supposed to be here anyway. What do you want?'

146

'Well, actually—' He rubbed his hand down his jeans with a little rasping sound. 'Actually to apologize. I think I might've spoken out of turn back there. No offence taken?'

He held out his hand.

'Let's leave it then,' Sister Joan said, not taking the hand.

'It's just I get sick of being made a laughing stock,' he said, letting his hand drop to his side. 'My own dad warned me that Dawn was a bit of a tart – a lot of a tart if you'll pardon the expression. And her family never took to me. Think I'm a bit of a dead loss all round. It's my nerves you see. Always was nervy since I was a kid. Brought up in Homes. Not wanted.'

'Mr Lurgan, you're still on convent property,' Sister Joan said coldly. 'If you have personal problems you must speak to someone professional.'

'I might get round to doing that. As long as you're not offended by my plain speaking?'

But everything about him offended her, she thought. The sandy hair, the pale eyes between their sparse lashes, the sinuous twist of his narrow shoulders as he levered himself from the stable door.

'If you'll excuse me,' she said, as civilly as she could muster, 'I really do have work to do. I can only repeat that you must seek some outside help. None of us is a trained counsellor. Good day.'

'I like horses. Like animals in general.'

He made no move to leave.

'I'm glad you do.'

'You've got a dog. I saw it running about in the grounds. I'd like to have a dog.'

'You would have to ask Mother David. I don't know if pets are permitted within the terms of the rental contract.'

'If that policewoman had had a dog she might not have been murdered.'

'Possibly. I really don't know.'

'She was very likely a waste of space anyway,' he said moodily, beginning to back away slightly. 'Most women are a waste of space. Take Winnie, my mother-in-law—'

'You take her, Mr Lurgan!' Sister Joan, finally losing patience, shut and locked the door against which he had recently been leaning and walked away, heading for the kitchen door.

She was half afraid that he would follow her but when she glanced round he had gone as silently as he had come.

'Was that one of the tenants you were talking to in the yard?' Sister Marie enquired.

'The son-in-law, Ian Lurgan. I told him he was out of bounds but he doesn't seem to hear what one says.'

'Probably fascinated because you're a nun,' Sister Marie said.

'Then he'd better get unfascinated very quickly.'

'You don't like him?'

'I don't know him. To be honest I don't particularly want to know any of them,' Sister Joan said.

'That's not like you, Sister.' There was faint disappointment in the younger woman's voice.

'I'm not sure what is *like me*,' Sister Joan said. 'All I know is that there's something terribly creepy about him. Do you need any help?'

'All done and dusted.'

'I'll go and take off my jeans before chapel.'

She went into the kitchen cell and closed the door, angry with herself for suddenly feeling so out of sorts and edgy.

Compassion, she thought, pulling down her jeans and smoothing the skirt of her grey habit, wasn't an easy virtue to practise.

'When you have a problem you cannot solve,' her own novice mistress had advised, 'then give it to God.'

Sister Joan knelt briefly before the plain wooden cross that comprised the only decoration in every cell.

'You deal with it then,' she said aloud, blessed herself hastily and joined the others as they made their way into chapel.

'Sister Joan.' Mother David detained her as they were coming out.

'Yes, Mother Prioress.'

'You know Police Constable Seldon was not a Catholic, so we are not obliged to attend her funeral or send a representative,' Mother David said. 'In fact I would have expected her to be buried in her home town, but her mother decided that since she chose to come here, though sadly for so brief a time, the interment will be here. I feel that it would be a nice gesture if someone from here was to go. If you feel inclined—? It is your own decision.'

'I hardly knew her at all,' Sister Joan said. 'However – yes, of course I'll go. You haven't heard—'

'How the investigation is proceeding? No, but if Inspector Mill requires your assistance then naturally you have my permission.'

'Thank you, Mother.'

She went upstairs to the refectory in a slightly happier mood.

'Sister Joan, there are some cheese tarts left over.' Sister Marie, clearing away before recreation, detained her.

'I can't think why. They were delicious,' Sister Joan said.

'Well, I like to make a few extra in case Luther comes around,' Sister Marie confessed. 'He was in the garden earlier on.'

'I'll take some to him before I join you,' Sister Joan said.

She slipped out and round into the garden, calling as she did so.

'Luther? Luther, are you there?'

It was dark enough to require a torch. Even as she hesitated, Luther answered her. 'Over here, Sister Joan! Just doing a lot of clearing up. We ought to have a bonfire.'

'That's Sister Martha's department. Sister Marie baked you some cheese tarts.'

'Lovely cheesy things she makes,' he commented, laying down his spade and approaching. 'Sister! Stand still!'

'What is it?' She teetered slightly, bag of tarts in her hand.

'There's one of them big slugs under your foot almost.'

He loped forward, stooped and picked up the slug, its mucus-covered body glistening whitely.

'Yuck! I can't stand them!' she said shiveringly.

'Not his fault he's a slug,' Luther said stolidly, placing the squirming creature out of harm's way. 'Mind you, I'd not make a pet of him neither.'

It was, she thought, an answer of sorts.

TWELVE

There was a considerable crowd at the funeral, probably because there was now a murder enquiry pending since Melanie Seldon had been too short a time in the town to have made any close friends.

Sister Joan, emerging after the simple Protestant service, stood aside as the coffin was borne from the church. Police officers from the Plymouth Force swelled the small police contingent from the town. In full uniform with a black band on his arm, Inspector Mill looked grave and remote. She guessed there would be plain-clothes men in the crowd, watching for anyone suspicious, anyone who, in the time-honoured tradition of killers, had come secretly to gloat.

She recognized Mrs Seldon more by instinct than anything else. The woman who had lost two children to unnatural death wore the traditional black to which she had added a red scarf as if to proclaim that she was not yet beaten by events. She had the same colour hair as her daughter, drawn back from a colourless face and tied with black ribbon at the nape of her neck. There was no sign of anyone who might've been Melanie's father.

There was obviously going to be no funeral repast. Mrs Seldon dropped a white rose on to the coffin, turned away and stood for a moment with head bowed and then straightened herself and moved proudly away, the inspector at her side.

'Sister Joan, may I introduce Mrs Seldon?' He paused where

she was standing. 'Mrs Seldon, Sister Joan met your daughter briefly. In the past she has been of great assistance to me in clearing up various cases. If you would like to come into the vicarage, the Reverend Mason has very kindly placed a room at our disposal.'

'You knew Melanie?' There was a note of eagerness in her voice.

'I met her very briefly on a couple of occasions,' Sister Joan said. 'She took my fingerprints for the purposes of elimination.'

'She was always most conscientious in her work,' Mrs Seldon said with a kind of dreary pride. 'If she had stayed in Plymouth she would have risen rapidly through the ranks. But she insisted on being transferred here.'

'Do you know why?' Sister Joan asked, as they began to walk up the path.

'She wasn't one to confide readily in people,' Mrs Seldon said. 'Ever since—' She hesitated for a moment, biting her lip, then went on, 'Perhaps you know that my son, Melanie's step-brother – half-brother I ought to say – committed suicide?'

'Yes, I heard about that.'

They were entering the rectory where a housekeeper ushered them into a study where tea and sandwiches were laid on a central table.

'Simon and Melanie were devoted,' Mrs Seldon said, accepting a cup of tea but shaking her head to the sandwiches. 'He was a quiet boy, sensitive, apt to be bullied you know, but Melanie always looked out for him. Always!'

'But things went wrong?' Asking the question Sister Joan noticed that Inspector Mill had seated himself slightly out of eye contact.

'He got in with the wrong type of people,' Mrs Seldon said. 'I don't mean criminal or anything like that! Rather silly young people who liked to dress up as Goths – stringy black hair and black nail varnish and purple eyeshadow and stuff like that – the boys as well as the girls. Not that Simon ever did! We wouldn't've allowed that, but he seemed fascinated by them, used to skip school and hang round the amusement arcade near the pier. His grades began to suffer.'

'Did you notice anything else unusual at that time?' Sister Joan asked.

'Oh, there was an outbreak of vandalism in the city,' Mrs Seldon said. 'Not unusual these days anywhere. Nothing too serious at first, just rude words chalked on boards, some cats went missing too if I recall – but I'm sure Simon had nothing to do with that. He liked animals.'

'Drugs?'

'He smoked cannabis once. He admitted it to me and said that it made him feel sick. You don't think that he was actually involved in selling? No, he would never have done that. Never!'

'But the wood where he – where he was found was used by the druggies?'

'It's just a bit of a wood really,' Mrs Seldon said. 'I mean it used to be a lovely spot for picnics in the summer. There were bluebells there too in the spring. A carpet of blue. Then some of the trees got some kind of fungal disease and people started dumping their rubbish.'

'And Simon still went there?'

'To see his mates he said, but they weren't boys I knew. He had stopped meeting the boys he knew, lost interest in football – he used to love football. Sister – Joan, is it? Yes, Sister Joan, do you think that whoever killed Melanie had something to do with Simon's death?'

'I've no idea,' Sister Joan said. 'But I think it possible that your daughter might've been following some plan of her own when she transferred down here.'

'It was an overnight thing,' Mrs Seldon said. 'She never told me what was in her mind. Then she said she was moving into Cornwall, that she thought she might like a change to a smaller place.'

'Did you hear from her after she moved?'

'She rang a couple of times just to say she had a nice place to stay and that the work at the station was very interesting.'

'I see. Thank you.' Sister Joan glanced at Inspector Mill.

'This has been a terrible ordeal for you,' he said, rising and coming to take a nearer chair.

'It hasn't quite sunk in yet,' she confessed.

'Nothing in any diaries or papers she left at home that might offer some clue?'

'I haven't had chance to look properly yet. Melanie didn't keep a diary as far as I know. Or she might have destroyed them or brought them with her. She is – *was* a grown woman.'

'Boy-friends?'

'Now and then. She wasn't the kind who went round in a crowd. She was always a bit of a loner – serious-minded.'

'The autopsy,' he said carefully, 'showed that she was still a virgin.'

'So she wasn't—?'

'No.'

'That's a comfort,' Mrs Seldon said on a long sigh. 'She always used to say that she was saving herself for the right man to come along. I'm thankful it wasn't—' She paused, a series of small dry sobs breaking from her.

'You ought to try to eat something,' Sister Joan said gently.

'I have to catch my train.' She had controlled herself again and was beginning to rise.

'I've arranged for a car to take you back to Plymouth. The police officers who came—'

'Offered to bring me,' she nodded, 'but I needed a space to be alone, to compose myself. If they have space—'

'If you'd like to come with me?'

'Thank you, Inspector Mill.' She turned and forced a watery smile in Sister Joan's direction. 'I'm sorry I wasn't able to be more help.'

'Again, my condolences,' Sister Joan said gravely.

This was not a moment for facile consolation.

'Back in a moment,' Alan Mill said.

Sister Joan nodded, standing by the window to watch them

as they walked down the path to the car and a knot of waiting officers.

Melanie Seldon, she mused, had come down into Cornwall for a specific purpose and it was almost certainly connected with the suicide of her half-brother. But why here? Why now? And why pursue whatever she had in mind without recourse to the proper authorities.

'Nice lady.' Inspector Mill re-entered.

'Brave, too. Alan, is there any further word from the autopsy?'

'She was killed in her bedsit,' he said.

'When?'

'Monday or Tuesday night. She had a day off on Tuesday but nobody seems to have seen her in town. She hadn't asked for extra leave which is why we were rather put out at the note that was left.'

'Which she neither wrote nor delivered.'

He nodded, sinking into a chair, nodding towards the table.

'Do us a favour and pour out a couple of cups of tea,' he said.

'Her bedsit was very neat and tidy.' She poured tea carefully.

'Someone had obviously cleaned it up, though as I say there wouldn't have been much blood. They took the cover off the mattress and turned it. We found a bloodstain – her blood – on the underside.'

'She was already in bed then? How did they – he get in?'

'A child could've opened that door,' he said. 'A credit card and a bit of jiggery-pokery and you can get into the shop and up to the first floor.'

'Surely there's a burglar alarm? There are some valuable—'

'The old fellow who runs the shop has been off all week with a cold. He hasn't been open for business at all. He rang Constable Seldon on her mobile and asked her to set the alarm for him. That was on Monday afternoon. She was in the office then, round about lunchtime so she'd've been alone.'

'And she didn't set it? Why not?'

He shrugged tiredly.

'Perhaps she forgot. I admit that seems unlikely since she struck me as a conscientious young woman, but it's possible if she had other things on her mind.'

'The figure I saw climbing over the wall,' Sister Joan said.

'*Thought* you saw.'

'Thought I saw – no, I *did* see it. I was blinded by the torch, that's all. It could have been her.'

'Then what the blazes was she doing trespassing in the convent grounds after dark?' he queried.

'I don't know. It was a black cloak, with a hood.'

'Sounds exactly like the one she was wrapped in.'

'And her outer garments. When she was taken from the river she was only wearing some undergarments under the cloak.'

'If she was killed late Monday night, which I feel is the more likely time,' he said slowly, 'she must have just got home. She took off her uniform.'

'Have you found it?'

'Not a trace. If we came across that it would be a valuable lead. Anyway she took off her uniform and maybe she lay down on the bed. If she'd just been climbing walls and speeding across the moor she'd be out of breath at the least. She might've dozed off.'

'Leaving the burglar alarm switched off?'

'Even police officers can forget. Anyway, whoever got in surprised her. If she was lying on her stomach the first blow would almost certainly have killed her. If there was a struggle then everything was tidied away nicely before he left.'

'Carrying Melanie Seldon over his shoulder?'

'This is a quiet street where the shop is,' he reminded her. 'Not many people around on a Monday night and the street itself isn't too far from the quay. There are boats moored there. Someone could have taken one down-river and dumped the body – it was weighted with stones – into the water. Then all they had to do was row the boat back and moor it again. A few people like to go night fishing so if anyone did see it—!

'The boats have been checked?'

'One of the first things we did. Nothing.'

'And the next step?'

'Patient police investigation,' he said wryly. 'You know there are very few unsolved murders in this country. Once we have the motive—'

'Her half-brother's suicide.'

'I agree with you. She was following an agenda of her own. One reason I wanted you to talk to her mother was because I wanted your own personal impression of Mrs Seldon.'

'A very respectable woman,' Sister Joan said slowly. 'She was obviously still in deep shock but endeavouring to control herself, to begin to come to terms with what had happened.'

'Religious?'

'I can't judge anyone's spiritual state!' Sister Joan exclaimed. 'At a guess I'd say she goes to church on feast days, doesn't gossip with her neighbours, believes in being respectable.'

'Not the kind of woman to drive her own son to suicide then?'

'I wouldn't have thought so. She obviously talked to Simon, tried to keep an eye on what he was getting up to.'

'No outside help?'

'She'd want to keep it in the family. Look, I really ought to go! I've the van here.'

'Thanks anyway. Good to get another point of view.'

At the door she turned.

'What was the other reason you wanted me here?' she asked.

'I like having you around,' he said, and drank his tea.

There were still a few people hanging round in the graveyard as the sexton filled in the hollow space. A couple of police officers still lingered, enclosed in a tight little knot of officialdom. She climbed into the van and drove back towards the convent, slowing and stopping as she saw Brother Cuthbert outside the former schoolhouse.

'I hear there's been another sudden death, Sister.' His normally beaming smile was conspicuous by its absence.

'Melanie Seldon, the new policewoman here, was killed,' Sister Joan said.

'Padraic Lee walked over to tell me about it, also to show me his new dog.'

'Kushti.'

'It was very thoughtful of Father Stephen to give the dog to him. I am always so pleased when I see evidence of kindness.'

'There wasn't much goodwill shown to Constable Seldon,' Sister Joan said bleakly.

'Alas no!' His face creased with distress. 'I have felt for some time, Sister, that evil was creeping closer. Felt it but not been able to pinpoint where it would strike.'

'Is that why you went to the postulancy?' she asked bluntly.

'No, I really did wonder if there was anything I could do to help make it ready for the tenants,' he assured her. 'But at the back of my mind was a creeping unease, as if my subconscious kept pace with what was threatening.'

'And the postulancy? Did you feel it there?'

'I only stayed a moment and then you arrived,' he said. 'No, that building is suffused with the goodness of Sister Hilaria. But who can tell where wickedness will lodge?'

'Mrs Pearson put candles there. Odd home-made candles.'

'She was a witch, wasn't she?'

'But not a bad person!'

'Wicca predates Christianity,' he said calmly. 'Many of its adherents are some of the holiest people around but every coin has another side. We ourselves had the Inquisition. A terrible blot on the Faith. How Our Dear Lady must've grieved over those poor souls dragged to the stake!'

'Brother Cuthbert, I think Mrs Pearson felt evil coming too,' Sister Joan said. 'I think that was why she put the candles there to try to protect the building, and later on she lit them in her bedroom to try to save herself from evil.'

'And whatever came into her room frightened her to death.'

'Melanie Seldon was struck over the head and thrown into the river. There was no accident or mischance about that!'

'Yes.' He was silent for a moment as if considering. Then he said briskly, 'Well, if evil is here we must fight it, each in his or her own way. Of course prayer is the safest course, but sometimes when an unlawful deed has been committed then practical action must be taken.'

'Do you think it could've been something – not of this world that so terrified Mrs Pearson she had a heart attack and died?' she asked.

'I would call it in the highest degree unlikely,' he returned. 'Satan and his minions are far too busy corrupting souls to have time for Mrs Pearson. No, I would say human agency was involved, people or a person vowed to evil.'

'Or simply led astray?' She shivered slightly.

'You cannot be led astray by evil,' he said. 'Evil must be invited in, must exact vows of loyalty and service. The great majority of criminals are not evil at all, just misguided and insensitive.'

'And now I must go and pray,' she said. 'We renew our vows soon and that means thinking about them.'

'I had forgotten! What a treat that will be for you all!'

'I hope so,' she said uncertainly, and went back to the van.

On impulse, she drove past the main gate along the external track that bordered the enclosure walls. As she neared the gate at the side of the old postulancy she was waved down, Mrs Roye having edged her bulk into the road.

'Good afternoon, Mrs Roye.'

'Always busy, Sister!' She heaved herself to the side of the vehicle.

'I try to be,' Sister Joan said.

'Pity you can't drum that into my son-in-law's head,' Mrs Roye said. 'Bone idle and never washes his feet! What my Dawn has to endure would try the patience of a saint! But you can't teach these young ones anything, can you? You haven't seen my Kit around?'

'I'm afraid not.'

'Went off in the car and hasn't come back yet. Henry was with her and I did hope that they'd shift themselves. Gone to that amusement arcade, I daresay! Nasty, germy place! But then my Kit's entitled to a spot of recreation and Henry likes to watch the girls.'

'I beg your—? How much longer is Mr del Marco staying?'

'Oh, he's looking round,' Mrs Roye said vaguely. 'Thinking of settling here for a bit. Quite a globetrotter is Henrico!'

'Yes, well. . . .' Sister Joan nodded as she clasped the steering-wheel again.

'I hear there's been a murder,' Mrs Roye said. 'It was in the local paper that Dawn bought last week. Some police officer. You don't expect murders in a place like this, do you?'

'I fear murders can occur anywhere,' Sister Joan said. 'You didn't go to the funeral?'

'Didn't know her, did I? Curiosity seekers go to funerals when a murder's been committed. I hate curiosity seekers! You went, did you?'

'Mother David felt that we ought to send a representative, yes. Good afternoon, Mrs Roye.'

'Had a bit of good news if you can call it that,' Mrs Roye said, not moving on. 'Tim Lurgan, Ian's father, is coming down to visit. All the way from dear old Liverpool!'

'But Mrs Roye—'

'Staying for a few days,' the other went on. 'Hopefully, he'll shake some sense into that idle lad of his, but who knows? Nice talking to you, Sister!'

The old postulancy was becoming somewhat crowded, Sister Joan reflected, as she drove on and reached by roundabout ways the yard.

'Was it very dreadful?' Sister Marie asked, as she went into the kitchen.

'Sad and respectable,' Sister Joan told her. 'There were

some people from the town there and some policemen. I met Mrs Seldon. She was very calm, very brave but obviously deeply shocked.'

'Poor lady!' Sister Marie blessed herself.

'I'd better go and report to Mother David before religious studies.'

'Did you want a cup of tea?'

'I had one at the vicarage. It was a very pleasant service.'

She went past the infirmary and tapped on the parlour door, opening it as she heard a murmur within.

Sister Gabrielle was seated at the desk immersed in some legal-looking documents.

'Is Mother sick?' Sister Joan asked.

'No no, she had a slight headache that's all,' Sister Gabrielle said, putting the papers back in the drawer. 'I was just . . . looking up some information, nothing that can't wait! I'd better go and prepare for religious studies. Perhaps you would man the telephone until Mother David comes down?'

'Yes, of course, Sister.'

She seated herself at the desk with a puzzled frown. Sister Gabrielle, stomping out with her stick, would not normally have been the one called to fill in on the rare occasions the prioress was sick or called away for a while. And she had asked nothing about the funeral.

Neither was Mother David in the habit of asking anyone to man the telephone, any more than Sister Dorothy had been during her term as prioress.

She slid open the top drawer and looked at the documents that Sister Gabrielle had put there. They seemed to be photocopies of census forms. Some local research the old lady was engaged on. Sister Gabrielle was a great one for crossword puzzles, quizzes and acrostics.

'Keeps the mind sharp and at nearly ninety,' she had been heard to proclaim, 'one needs to work at it. Now, can anyone tell me who Brad Pitt is? Sounds like a footballer.'

Sister Joan dropped the papers back in the drawer and put

her chin in her hands.

None of Winifred Roye's brood had gone to watch the funeral. She would have guessed if asked that they were the kind of people who would turn up to gawp at funerals and accidents, which just showed, she mused with a sigh, how snobbish she was getting!

Yet of all the people who might have rented the old postulancy they struck her as the most unlikely to fit in, whatever their priest had said.

On impulse she opened the drawer again and pushed the census forms aside. Underneath was the square white pad on which telephone numbers were jotted down together with time and duration of calls. There was no date or time marked by the number of Father John Fitzgerald.

Mother David and the now Sister Dorothy had gone on the recommendations in his letter then.

If she stopped to think she wouldn't do it! She picked up the receiver and dialled the number on the pad.

The ringing went on for about half a minute before it was cut off by a voice saying briefly, 'Yes?'

'May I speak to Father John Fitzgerald, please?' she asked.

'Father John speaking. Who is this?'

'I'm calling from the Convent of Our Lady of Compassion.'

'No problems with your new tenants I hope?' He sounded worried. 'Mrs Roye is not a healthy woman, bad heart you know, unhappily finds it hard to shed weight. An affliction from which many of us suffer!'

'No, she's perfectly well,' Sister Joan said. 'I wondered if they had informed you that they got here safely – there's no telephone in the old postulancy.'

'Ian Lurgan called on his mobile, said they were very comfortable. Are you the prioress? I wrote to a Mother Dorothy.'

'I'm manning the telephone. She isn't feeling very well.'

'I'm sorry to hear that. Well, you can assure her that I am aware the family has settled in. Rough round the edges but hearts of gold all of them. Was there anything else, Sister?'

'Thank you, no. Good bye, Father.'

She hung up quickly and took a couple of deep breaths. Well. Winifred Roye and her family were perfectly ordinary people save for being a bit rough round the edges. In any case things had begun to go wrong at least a fortnight before they'd travelled to Cornwall. She was letting her imagination get the better of her, a fault she hoped she had managed to eradicate.

'Sister Joan, what on earth are you doing?' Mother David's voice interrupted her musing.

'Sister Gabrielle asked me to man the telephone since you were feeling unwell.'

'I do not know,' Mother David said testily, 'what has got into Sister Gabrielle the last few days. I had a very slight headache and she insisted it was about to turn into a full blown migraine and that I must go and lie down. The post had just come and I was about to sort it but she was so insistent – God bless her but she has such excellent intentions. I hope you're not think-ing of sitting at my desk all day, Sister.'

'I'm sorry, Mother!' Sister Joan hastily vacated her seat.

Mother David glanced at her watch.

'I will sort out the post later on,' she said. 'We'd best start religious studies. I believe I advised ten minutes' meditation before we discussed the importance of believing in the internal truths of the vows we take. Come along, Sister!'

Sister Joan followed meekly. Out of the corner of her eye as they turned into the chapel she was aware of Sister Gabrielle coming slowly from the infirmary and equally aware that if she looked in the desk again the census papers would have gone.

THIRTEEN

'Tabitha, how are you?'

Sister Joan, dismounting from Lilith and with Alice gambolling at her heels, waved to the girl who was walking up the track.

'Hello, Sister.' Tabitha's greeting was less than enthusiastic.

'Been shopping? You've never walked all the way from town?'

The girl who was carrying two shopping bags shrugged.

'Look, if you like,' Sister Joan said, determined to ignore the other's surliness, 'I can put your baskets on Lilith and take them over to the camp for you. It isn't much out of my way.'

'I can manage, thanks,' Tabitha said curtly.

'Well, if you're sure – is Edith catching you up?'

'She's at home with Dad,' Tabitha said. 'I don't have her tagging after me every place you know.'

'No, of course not. Younger siblings can be a bit trying sometimes, can't they?' Sister Joan said, recalling her two brothers.

'She's all right,' Tabitha said, flicking back a long plait of hair. 'See you!'

She went off, her red-ribboned braids bouncing against the back of her anorak.

She probably thinks I'm an interfering busybody, Sister Joan thought wryly. After all what does a nun know about being fifteen?

165

She shook her head slightly at her own intolerance. Padraic Lee had mentioned he was worried about his older daughter, but the Roms were strict with their children. Tabitha, she thought, was probably just going through a difficult stage.

October had come in with the kind of crisp, sunlit weather that almost banished the memory of the windy September. Her spirits lifted as she tossed a stick for Alice and felt the wind tugging at her short curly hair as it strayed from beneath the band of her veil – not a wet, spiteful wind, but a playful breeze that lifted her spirits.

'Playing hookey?'

Inspector Mill, driving towards her, braked and put his head out of the window.

'I wish!' she retorted. 'No, with winter ahead I try to give Lilith as much exercise as I can. You've news?'

'We've found a witness,' he said. 'Not a particularly law-biding one unfortunately. A local poacher was skirting around the alleys waiting for his mate who didn't after all turn up. He says there was a fellow at the shop door of the antique shop, and then the front door opened and a young woman let him in.'

'Constable Seldon!' Sister Joan exclaimed.

'He saw her silhouetted against the light and gave us a pretty good description – slim, blonde hair, wearing a dark cloak. The man went in and closed the door and then he heard some people coming so he went off, decided to go home and watch TV.'

'What was the visitor like?' she asked.

'He didn't get more than a glimpse – long dark overcoat and one of those trilby hats on.'

'When did this happen?'

'Late on Monday a fortnight back. He reckoned it was about ten-thirty or eleven.'

'It was earlier when I saw the figure come over the enclosure wall,' she said. 'Alan, that must've been Constable Seldon! She shone her torch because she didn't want to be recognized and made off across the moor before I could gather my wits!'

'But what was she doing in that particular spot? She certainly wasn't on official police business,' he said, unhappily. 'I reckon she had an agenda of her own concerning her half-brother's suicide. Anyway it confirms that her death did take place on the Monday.'

'But still wearing her cloak hours later?'

'I'll tell you what I reckon.' He opened the car door and swung his long legs to the side. 'I've no idea why she fixed on the convent walls to go snooping but she did, then you drove along and she flashed her torch and ran like hell over the moors. When she got back to her bed-sit she was probably tired and grubby, so she stripped off, took a bath or a shower, put her underwear back on and was about to reach for a robe and have a hot drink or something when the front doorbell sounded. She grabbed the first thing to hand, the cloak, and went downstairs to let the visitor in.'

'Just after she'd been climbing over the—? Surely not!'

'I doubt if she imagined for a moment that anyone had actually followed her, or that whoever she was investigating would turn up at her door within a couple of hours,' he said wryly. 'I wish our sole witness had stayed behind a minute longer – he might've seen the so-called visitor shove her backwards as he stepped in.'

'How do you know she was shoved?' Sister Joan demanded.

'A couple of strands of blonde hair caught in the sharp corner of a walnut table a few feet inside the shop door,' he told her. 'It's my educated guess that he did shove her and that she fell heavily. Then whoever it was shut the shop door, carried her upstairs, put her on her bed – she had already turned back the covers ready for getting into bed – and she must have died there since the intruder turned the mattress but failed to notice the slight stain of blood on it.'

'You're trying to tell me it wasn't murder!'

'That'd be for a jury to decide. In my book it's murder. He then put the cloak tightly round her, collected all the papers and private notes and her uniform and carried her down to one of the boats.'

'Then he'd've been a pretty strong man – you're assuming it was a man?'

'I'm assuming nothing,' he said drily. 'Anyway she was slim, certainly not very heavy.'

'But it couldn't've been the same man who dressed in her uniform and calmly walked into the police station on Wednesday morning to leave a note!'

'Oh, I think he had some help,' Detective Inspector Mill said, grimly.

'Are you going to question our tenants?' Sister Joan asked. 'They weren't here when any of the earlier events occurred.'

'Maybe there was no connection – no, there has to be.'

'The obscene writings and sketches you saw.'

'And destroyed or obliterated,' she said contritely.

'The normal human instinct is to clean away dirt. Don't fret yourself about it,' he advised. 'No, the incidents seemed to me to be like the prelude to something bigger. The sketches, the poisoned lurcher, the drowned cat, and I'm not forgetting the figure capering in the graveyard with the obvious intention of frightening an old lady out of her wits!'

'But you'll question the new tenants anyway?' she repeated.

'I've no reason to go barging in. There's no foreign DNA been found that would justify the expense of a general inquiry. These tenants, Sister? What do you make of them? You've talked to them?'

'I don't like them,' she said flatly.

'It's not like you to be judgemental. Describe them.'

'The mother is a widow called Winifred Roye,' she said. 'About sixty-five or thereabouts – fat – not just plump or well built, but fat. You get the impression that if you pricked her she'd leak lard. Very fond of her daughter, Dawn Lurgan. Dawn's about thirty, dresses like a – well, young women with thick thighs ought to lower their skirts – sorry if that sounds catty – but in ten years she—'

'Will look as fat as her mother,' she was interrupted.

His voice was vaguely amused.

'Yes,' Sister Joan said bluntly. 'She is married to Ian Lurgan, Aged about thirty, smallish, thin, nondescript really, has an ingratiating manner and obviously never talked to a nun in his life before.'

'He doesn't seem to have ingratiated himself with you.'

'No, he hasn't. He hangs around, won't take the hint to be off. He followed me into the stable yard and that's off limits to the tenants anyway, and spent the entire conversation bad-mouthing his wife for her immoral habits.'

'There's a sister, isn't there?'

'Kit. About twenty, I'd say. Tall, good-looking girl, red hair, rather rude.'

'In what way?'

'Oh, it's stupid of me to mind!' she said impatiently. 'Nuns grow accustomed to being treated with a kind of friendly respect. She tried to wind me up by being deliberately insolent.'

'And there's a visitor?'

'Henrico del Marco, but he hasn't got an Italian accent. Of course, he may have been born in this country of Italian parentage. In his early to mid-forties, thickset, looks powerful. But surely you've made some enquiries?'

'I rang Mother David and asked her for the number of their referee. A Father John Fitzgerald. Sounded like a nice fellow.'

'You talked to him?'

'He told me they were a rough family, had a hard time of it since the father died. He didn't know of any criminal record. Said he would certainly have heard since they were parishioners of his.'

'Have they been to Mass since they got here?'

'I had a word with Father Malone. He hasn't noticed any new communicants – but it isn't illegal to skip church.'

'I suppose not. What happens now?'

'There'll be the inquest and, unless we can come up with

169

some new evidence, a verdict of unlawful killing by person or persons unknown.'

He shrugged tiredly and swung his legs back inside the car.

'I'm worried about Tabitha Lee,' she said abruptly.

'She hasn't started hitting people over the head, has she?'

'Not as far as I know – no, of course not! But she's started skipping classes, hanging around in the amusement arcade. Padraic frets about her.'

'Padraic Lee's an excellent father,' Inspector Mill said. 'I daresay she is just going through a phase. They tell me girls do.'

'Not boys?'

'Brian and Keith? Not yet, but I'm keeping my fingers crossed.' He laughed, the shadow lifting from his face.

'And the – rest of the family?'

'All present and correct! Will you be coming to the inquest?'

'To give evidence about the cloaked figure I saw?'

'I'll have a word with the coroner and find out if you'll be needed. One glimpse on a dark evening, unsubstantiated by witnesses, is not going to make any difference to the verdict, but we'll see. It's certain that she died late on the Monday night.'

'And walked into the station to leave a note on the Wednesday morning?'

'Someone dressed in her uniform. Who hasn't turned up yet. I want to get this thing wrapped up by the end of the month.'

'Any particular reason?' she asked.

'All Saints' Day on the first, All Souls' Day on the second, and Guy Fawkes on the fifth. I suppose you lot don't celebrate it?'

'I can't speak for the laity,' she said, amused, 'but we don't have bonfires to mark the occasion in the convent, no. I didn't know you were *au fait* with church ceremonies!'

'Protestants have them too,' he reminded her.

'Of course they do! How arrogant of me!'

'Don't worry about it. You're talking to one who is strictly neutral here,' he said.

'Were you on your way to the convent?'

'To fill Mother David in on the details so far. I spend so much time on the phone that it's a relief to talk face to face. Anyway perhaps you can pass on the news to your prioress?'

'Of course I will.'

'And Sister—'

'Yes?'

'This spate of nastiness may have stopped, but if I were you I'd keep alert.'

'I've taken to locking the stable door at night and keeping Alice in the kitchen after dark unless someone's with her.'

'Of course,' he said with a faint smile. 'I was concerned about the welfare of the animals. Bye, Sister!'

He turned the car in a wide arc and drove off down the hill.

'Come on, Lilith! Alice!'

She was remounting when Padraic Lee strode into view. At his heels the new lurcher frolicked, immediately sensing a play-mate in Alice who, having sniffed the newcomer carefully, evidently decided that a game of tag was in order.

'She looks well!' Sister Joan said, dismounting again.

'Aye, she's a nice dog,' Padraic agreed. 'Pedigree too! Father Stephen gave Edith the proper forms all signed and sealed.'

He dug into his jacket and produced a couple of sheets of typed matter.

'Father Stephen signed on my behalf – not that I can't read or write, but some folk take it for granted that all Roms are illiterate,' he said, handing them over.

'Very impressive,' Sister Joan said.

Her eye scanning the neatly typed details of sire and dam, of injections given, lit on the signature with the n at the end of *Stephen* flourishing backwards in a reverse loop.

'Aye, she's a right good bitch!' Padraic said, taking back the papers and stowing them away carefully. 'Kushti! Heel, now! Heel now!'

'Is Edith well?'

'Both of them are fine.'

'I saw Tabitha earlier. Did she get the shopping home all right. I did offer to—'

'She's not home yet.' He looked slightly puzzled. 'She had some debating society to stay for. Edith weren't sure what it was. And we got in all the shopping on Saturday.'

'I must've been mistaken then,' Sister Joan said lamely.

'I'd best be getting on. Training time!'

He nodded and went off, the puppy scampering at his heels.

'Alice! Here!'

To her surprise Alice obeyed instantly, panting up and sitting down with an expression on her face that said clearly, 'When it comes to obedience that lurcher can't hold a candle to me'.

Why had Tabitha been carrying two laden baskets? Mounting up again, Sister Joan felt a spasm of unease. No shopping? Things for Guy Fawkes Night perhaps? Time she stopped putting a sinister construction on every little incident.

She had almost reached the gates of the convent when the neat little car swept around the corner with Dawn Lurgan at the wheel. At her side a smartly dressed elderly man, bearing, Sister Joan noticed, a decided resemblance to Ian Lurgan, turned his head and stared at her before saying something to the young woman beside him who, clearly reluctantly, slowed and stopped.

'This is Ian's father,' Dawn said, winding down the window at the side. 'We're going into town to get a fish and chip supper.'

'Sister Joan.' She remained on Lilith but nodded pleasantly.

'Tim,' the newcomer muttered. 'Name's Tim.'

'Right! Let's get on, babe! Nice seeing you, Sister!'

She shot past, causing Lilith to rear nervously.

So that was Ian's father. Rather careworn and nervous-looking, she decided, and who could blame him with Ian for a son?

'Charity, charity!' she said aloud, calming the pony.

'And thats all of it, Mother David.'

Twenty minutes later she completed her recital of Inspector Mill's news and sat back on her stool.

'One hopes that the police will apprehend the guilty party,' Mother David said worriedly. 'What a burden to have on one's conscience! Perhaps the weight of his conscience will drive him to confess.'

'Perhaps,' Sister Joan said, trying to put some agreement into her voice.

In her experience criminals were seldom bothered by their consciences.

'You have a little time before religious studies,' Mother David said. 'Father Malone phoned to say that both he and Father Stephen have this nasty chill that is apparently going about so for once chapel and benediction are cancelled. We shall use that period for private meditation on the renewal of our vows. How are the sketches coming?'

'Rather well, Mother,' Sister Joan said. 'Saint Ignatius Loyola is rather a handsome warrior.'

'Which I suppose children will find rather more exciting than his later spiritual conversion. Thank you, Sister. *Dominus vobiscum.*'

'*Et cum spiritu tuo,*' Sister Joan responded.

She went across into the chapel and climbed the spiral stairs to the library above. Sister Dorothy was at the main desk, head bent over a book.

'I took the liberty of looking at some of your sketches,' she said, looking up. 'They are really delightful. I begin to feel guilty that during my time as prioress I rather discouraged your artistic interests.'

'It was very good for my soul, Sister Dorothy,' she answered encouragingly, and went on into the storeroom.

Her drawings were pinned up, the light when she switched it on bringing the ones she had coloured to glowing life.

There they were, she thought, waiting to be translated into

173

printed books. Anne building a castle of bricks with her grandson, Jesus; Bernadette at the spring; Christopher carrying the Christ Child across the river; David taking a modest shower; Elizabeth with her basket of roses; Francis surrounded by small animals; George with his rather impudent looking dragon; Hildegard singing and playing; Ignatius in his Spanish armour; her namesake mounted on her horse with the fleur-de-lis borne before her – it was hard not to feel a glow of satisfaction.

She added a few touches here and there, then mindful that she still had to join the meditation which replaced the religious studies, she switched off the light and joined Sister Dorothy who was on her way down the spiral stairs to kneel in her accustomed place.

They were filing in, Sister Marie with a large dab of flour on her nose. Mother David came in, made her usual neat genuflection and turned to face them.

'Sisters, I owe you an apology for postponing our religious studies to a later date,' she said. 'Sometimes the world intrudes too much and naturally though we are not living in the world we are still of it. Because of recent events I took the unusual step of ordering all the local and a couple of the national newspapers in order to fully acquaint myself with what has been happening beyond our enclosure. The nastiness, if I may call it that, seems to be endemic, spreading like a cancer. In every town there seem to be random acts of violence against the aged and weak, even against children. In view of that, I have decided to ask the Mother House if we may donate one-third of any rental we receive from any property to a children's organization. I believe we will receive that permission, but I will not take such an unusual step without consulting – where is Sister Gabrielle?' She broke off, looking round the chapel where only a few candles mitigated the gloom.

'She was in the infirmary before, Mother,' Sister Mary Concepta piped up.

'Perhaps she dozed off. Shall I fetch her?' Sister Perpetua was on her feet.

'Normally I would prefer not to disturb her,' Mother David said, 'but when it comes to making economic decisions then Sister Gabrielle must also be consulted.'

'I won't be a minute. Please excuse me, Sisters.'

Sister Perpetua went out, her tread echoing on the bare wood of the hall.

'Sister?' Mother David spoke questioningly as the tall figure of the infirmarian returned.

'Sister Gabrielle isn't in the infirmary, Mother David,' she said.

'Sister Mary Concepta, was Sister Gabrielle actually in the infirmary when you came into chapel?' Mother David asked.

'She was there earlier today,' Sister Mary Concepta said, her voice suddenly uncertain. 'Sister Perpetua gave me my heart pills at four and – she was there then, wasn't she?'

'Seated by the fire,' Sister Perpetua confirmed. 'I went into the kitchen to ask Sister Marie for something or other—'

'And I had a little sleep,' Sister Mary Concepta said. 'Those pills are very relaxing. When I heard the rest of you coming into chapel I roused myself and joined you. I don't know whether she was still there or not.'

'Would she be in the bathroom upstairs?' Sister Martha said.

'Why would she go upstairs when there's a perfectly adequate bathroom and toilet in the infirmary? Sister Marie, go and see if she's in the parlour. She may have fallen.'

'May I help?' Sister Katherine asked.

'Yes, go along! She certainly won't be out of doors,' Mother David said.

They sat in a strained silence for the next five minutes until the two sisters came back in, their faces expressing frustration.

'We've looked everywhere,' Sister Marie said. 'Mother David, she isn't in the building anywhere.'

FOURTEEN

'May I make a suggestion?' Sister Dorothy was rising to the occasion, unconsciously asserting her old habit of authority.

'That we divide up and search?' Mother David said.

'You have anticipated me, Mother Prioress.' Sister Dorothy gracefully relinquished the habit of authority again.

'This is a large building,' Mother David said, pushing back her spectacles and frowning in concentration. 'Sisters Katherine and Marie, search the upper floor very thoroughly: Sister Dorothy, will you search the library and storerooms and then join Sisters Hilaria and Mary Concepta in the parlour with me. I shall wait there in case – if she has strayed beyond the enclosure – someone may have found her and be trying to reach us by telephone. In fact, when your particular search has been concluded each of you is to return to the parlour. Sister Perpetua, you had better remain in the infirmary once you have checked the ground floor. If Sister Gabrielle has gone out of doors for any reason she will be needing a hot drink when she returns. Sister Martha, take a torch and search the front grounds. Sister Joan, take Alice and cover the garden and the cemetery.'

They were filing out more rapidly than usual. Sister Joan reached for her cloak.

'She cannot have gone far,' Sister Martha said, reaching for her own garment. 'Sister Gabrielle never leaves the main house except to give Lilith the occasional sugar lump.'

'Elderly nuns don't vanish into thin air,' Sister Joan said briskly, 'and Sister Gabrielle is a bit of a law unto herself you know. If she took it into her head to walk barefoot to Rome I doubt if anyone could dissuade her.'

'You don't think—?'

'No, of course I don't! Here's a torch. If you run into Luther tell him what's happened.'

'Luther's nearly always gone by dusk,' Sister Martha said unhappily as she headed for the front door, 'and anyway we don't know what's happened.'

Sister Joan fished a second torch out of its drawer and went through to the yard. Alice, jumping from her basket, followed gaily, ears pricked.

'Keys!' Sister Joan fumbled for them and opened the stable door, surprising Lilith who stood half asleep in her stall.

'Sister Gabrielle?'

A cursory look convinced her that the other wasn't there. She whistled Alice into the yard again, locked the door, and walked on into the shrubbery, moving the circle of light from her torch from side to side as she called,

'Sister Gabrielle! Sister Gabrielle!'

There were no answers save the rustling of leaves and her own footsteps crunching stone and gravel and bits of bark dislodged by the recent winds.

Gardens, she thought, looked different by late twilight, the edges of the vegetable beds ringed with the first faint rays of the moon as it rose to vanquish the sun for a space, shadows purpling and creeping closer. She was aware of movement all about her as if the grass quivered in sympathy with the search. Even Alice, as if becoming aware of the situation, ceased gambolling and walked sedately at her heels.

The apple trees and pear trees, denuded of their harvest, cast crooked shadows over the fruit bushes where blackberries still lingered.

'Sister Gabrielle!'

She raised her voice, hearing it small and diminished in the silent spaces. The cemetery displayed a row of simple white crosses, each with a bunch of autumn daisies laid upon the turf that covered the uncoffined graves of former sisters.

'Sister Gabrielle!'

Alice gave a disgusted yelp and headed for home.

It was surely impossible for Sister Gabrielle to have walked so far. Not only impossible but in the highest degree unlikely, since she had frequently declared when, in the hotter months, the two oldest members of the community had taken short strolls in the grounds, that for her own part she saw no good in visiting the cemetery since before too long she'd be ending up there anyway!

She bent her torch downwards and moved to the steps that ran down to the old tennis court. The moon was strengthening now and she could discern the shadows of the posts and the remnants of net that lifted in a sudden breeze and writhed before they sank down again.

Had Sister Gabrielle gone over to the old postulancy? And if so, then why? What could've possessed her?

Switching off her torch altogether she went down the steps and across the court, skirting the fluttering remnants of net and rope.

The curtains were partly drawn and she could see Winifred Roye seated at the head of the table, eating what looked like fish and chips, her eyes fixed unblinkingly on her plate as she lifted forkfuls to her mouth.

'Hello, Sister.' The voice, sibilant and low, made her jump violently.

'Mr Lurgan!' She pronounced the name on a gasp.

'Sorry if I scared you, Sister,' he said.

'Actually,' she said, recovering her breath, 'I fear I might've startled you. I was – I am so used to taking a walk here that I – I must consider it out of bounds in future I suppose. My apologies!'

'You come whenever you like, Sister,' he said.

179

Now was the moment to enquire if he had seen Sister Gabrielle, but the words stuck in her throat. Instead she said lamely, 'I'd best round up Alice. Are you—?'

'Dawn forgot to fill up the tank,' he said, 'so she and Henry went on back into town to get some petrol. I decided to walk part of the way.'

'But you bought the fish and chips—?'

'Ate them quick and then went back down,' he said. 'The old trout's on her second full helping. One day she'll burst and we'll have to clean up her crap!'

'Yes, well, good evening, Mr Lurgan.'

As she turned on her heel his voice came softly through the moon-striped dark. 'I'd really like us to be friends, Sister. I don't have many friends, most of them do you down anyway! But I wish – sometimes I just wish I could get away.'

'From what?' She felt impelled to ask.

'From them.' His voice had dropped to a murmur. 'I'd give anything to be – I will one day, you just see if I don't! You just see!'

He had moved away silently before she could think of any reply, his thin frame slipping in and out of moonlight.

She ought to have asked him if he'd seen Sister Gabrielle but something had held her back. She turned away from the small building and went swiftly across the tennis court. Sister Gabrielle would never have walked this far and if by some chance she'd managed it then why would she come this way anyway?

The side gate was being pushed open. She moved into the shadow of the wall and watched them come through, he thick-set and predatory, she leaning against him, her hair pulled back into a tail to display her round pallid face. They stood for a moment, caught in a beam of moonlight in a grotesque embrace, and then moved again towards the house.

'Sister!'

The whisper came from the top of the steps.

The figure emerging from the shrubbery looked for one

instant like the cartoon outline of a witch, veil whipped side-ways, strands of hair silvered by the moonglow, cape billowing as the twigs snagged it, stick held almost parallel with the ground as if its owner intended to mount up and fly away.

'Sister Gabrielle? What on earth—?'

Sister Joan went up the steps to help her as the old lady straightened up.

'Keep your voice down!' Sister Gabrielle whispered. 'Sound travels after dark.'

'Sister, what happened to you?' Sister Joan hissed back. 'We are all out looking for you!'

'Very silly of you,' Sister Gabrielle said, planting the tip of her stick firmly in the earth and taking her younger companion's arm. 'I decided to take a walk, that's all. It seemed like a pleasant enough afternoon so I took a stroll. I went a little further than I intended and sat down to rest.'

'In the shrubbery?'

'They ought to provide a bench there you know for the older members of the community so that they can rest before going back. I fell asleep as it was, happily ensconced in a rather convenient grassy hollow.

'Then when I heard you calling I thought at first that I was still dreaming and it occurred to me that I might have caused a little trouble and inconvenience so I waited a few minutes and then I tried to get up, but getting up takes more energy at my age than sitting down. So! There you have it and I do beg pardon for causing any worry.'

'I see,' Sister Joan said, wishing she could believe every word of it.

'As it is,' Sister Gabrielle said, panting slightly, 'I shall have Mother David and Sister Perpetua to deal with. Dear good people but of the opinion that elderly ladies like flowers should be stuck in one place and left there!'

'It might have been more sensible to tell someone,' Sister Joan said. 'I mean, a walk is always a good idea but someone could've come with you.'

'Do you never have moments,' Sister Gabrielle said, pausing as they reached the enclosure proper, 'when you want to be out in the open air and entirely alone? Oh, why should you have? You are forever driving here and riding there! And of course one can be alone within the house but to stride out like a girl again – I used to be quite an energetic walker you know.'

'I'm sure you did.'

Sister Joan paused to give herself sufficient time to catch her breath. Sister Gabrielle seemed to have taken no harm from her escapade but she felt strongly that something more than a desire for a solitary ramble had taken the older nun out.

Cautiously she said, 'If you feel like a walk again then I'd be happy to come with you. I wouldn't intrude on your privacy. I could just stroll along behind.'

'Picking daisies and calling Alice and me to fetch a stick in turns, I suppose?' Sister Gabrielle snorted. 'You're a dear girl, Sister, but – but there are occasions when your practical sense seems to desert you. Now give me your arm again and I'll face the music. And whatever you do, when I'm gone, don't stick daisies on top of me!'

'Orchids perhaps?' Sister Joan suggested mischieviously.

'The convent budget wouldn't run to it,' Sister Gabrielle said. 'Slow down a little. Otherwise you'll be ordering orchids before we both know it!'

'You've found her!' Sister Perpetua came striding down from the yard. 'Gabrielle, where have you been? The entire house is in a state about you!'

'Sister Gabrielle took a walk and fell asleep,' Sister Joan said.

'And you took your time finding her!' Sister Perpetua said crossly. 'Oh, and Alice dashed off again the moment I called her in! Someone is teaching her bad habits!'

'I'll go and fetch her,' Sister Joan said, relinquishing Sister Gabrielle to the infirmarian's charge.

Alice would probably be back in the garden, hunting the odd imaginary rabbit. She turned the switch higher on her torch and called the dog's name in as coaxing a tone as her growing irritation would allow. There were times, and this was one of them, when she heartily sympathized with Sister Perpetua's sharpness of tongue.

'Alice, will you—?'

Alice came bounding up, tail waving energetically.

'You've really disgraced yourself this time,' she scolded. 'Some fine guard dog you are! No, it isn't time for a game!'

Alice, unheeding, was pawing her skirt with frantic paws.

'What is it?'

Her attention alerted she stood still, tracing with her torch the path that Alice took as she bounded away again.

'What is it, girl?'

Alice, half returning, whined again and ran off.

'All right! But if you're just being silly you can forget all about any games tomorrow,' she scolded, skirting a large patch of gooseberry bushes as she rounded a corner.

Luther had been busy clearing up the garden, piling up twigs and dead grass obviously in the hope of a bonfire. The mound looked like the hump of a half-buried camel in the torchlight.

Alice was engaged in tugging with her teeth at something that jutted out beyond the upper part of the heap.

'What is it?'

Sister Joan stooped to tug the object which resolved itself into a heap as the upper part of the mound slithered down.

She shone her torch, a quiver of shock running along her backbone. Brass buttons glinted in the light against the dark serge of a jacket and skirt, a white shirt, muddied beyond hope, lay next to a dark hat.

'Is anything wrong, Sister?' Luther had plodded across and stood looking down at her.

'Luther, how long have you been in the garden here?' She stood up and looked at him.

'I just got here, Sister,' he said. 'I was on the moor having a look round and I heard Sister Martha calling by the front gates. When Sister Martha calls I come running as you knows well,

Sister. She said Sister Gabrielle were gone. I said, "Well, 'tisn't likely she's run off to be wed!" and then we heard Sister Perpetua calling she was found and safe so I came round to the back to check on my bonfire heaps. You'm gone and messed that one up proper, Sister.'

'When did you make this heap?'

'Almost a week since. I keep adding bits and pieces I find.'

'You found these?' She shone the torch downwards again.

'No, Sister. That's policeman's belongings.'

'You didn't find them and put them on the heap here?'

'No, Sister. I just said.'

He had scowled, underlip jutting.

'Right! Luther, will you stay here and keep guard? Don't let a soul near it.'

'If Sister Martha comes I'd not want to be refusing her.'

'Sister Martha will be helping to look after Sister Gabrielle,' Sister Joan said, more patiently than she felt. 'Just wait here. I won't be long. And don't touch anything!'

She took to her heels and flew up to the yard.

'Sister Joan, where on earth have you been?' Sister Marie opened the back door, her round face flushed. 'Have you found Alice? She hasn't come back here and Sister Gabrielle said she wasn't with you and—'

'Is Sister Gabrielle all right?'

Sister Marie's face dimpled into a smile.

'Worn out but feisty as ever,' she said. 'Mother David is reading her the riot act in the parlour. What is it, Sister? You look a bit hot and bothered!'

'I'm probably having a nervous breakdown,' Sister Joan said grimly. 'Sister, as soon as Sister Gabrielle comes out of the parlour ask Mother David to telephone the police.'

'Something else has happened?'

'The clothes the policewoman had are on one of the heaps in the garden. Luther's standing guard! I need to find Alice!'

She went out again, leaving Sister Marie open-mouthed, and stopped short as she saw a tall figure loom into view, a wriggling dog under his arm.

'Padraic! Is Alice hurt?'

'No thanks to her that she isn't,' he said. 'She ran out almost under the wheels of my lorry about five minutes since.'

'You were coming here?'

The sudden suspicion that he might deal in more than a few illegal salmon stopped her short.

'Looking for Tabitha,' he said.

'But surely—? I saw her on her way to the camp.'

'She didn't turn up. Gone dancing, or down at those slot machines I thought, but when it got dark I started fretting. There's no bus up after the last school bus. I wondered if she'd gone walking on the moor since she wasn't anywhere in town. I asked a couple of her friends but they hadn't seen her since school came out. I left Edith with old Sarah, but she'll be fretting soon if I don't get back.'

'Look, Inspector Mill is probably on his way here—' Sister Joan began.

'About Tabitha? You know I don't hold with—'

'The police will find her if she's strayed away,' Sister Joan said quickly. 'It's my belief she's probably on her way back now, wondering what kind of reception she'll get.'

'I hope you're right, Sister,' he said moodily.

'Oh, so do I,' she agreed fervently. 'Padraic, why don't you drive up to the convent yourself and deliver Alice? I have something to do. You can ask if anyone has seen Tabitha since I saw her.'

She handed Alice back into the lorry, turned and sped towards the gardens.

Luther still stood by the mound of discarded junk, his stance as belligerent as if he expected an invading army to come storming through.

'The police are on their way,' she said, hoping that they were. 'Stay here a while longer.'

'Is Sister Martha all right?' he demanded.

'Sister Martha is just fine. You stay here now.'

She went on past the cemetery and along the shrubbery. She was moving by instinct but there were times when one trusted one's instinct.

The sleek little car was just nosing to its parking stop outside the side gate. She traversed the tennis court rapidly and stood in the shadow of the wall.

'Thank God that's done!' Kit Roye's voice came to her clearly.

'Think she'll do, babe?'

Her brother-in-law. Ian Lurgan, sounded slightly anxious as if he wasn't sure what reply to expect or want.

'Reckon so! And she's a gyppo so the pigs won't be too bothered about what she gets up to,' Kit Roye said.

'Leave it to the ones who know what they're doing, eh?'

'Yeah, babe!'

'Stop calling me that!' His voice was suddenly petulant.

'You think Dawn'd mind? She's probably shacked up with your dad by now if Henry hasn't taken all the bed space. Oh, do get on!'

The gate clanged shut. If either of them turned they would surely see her, standing motionless against the wall.

The front door of the old postulancy opened, they went in, the door closed. The downstairs light went off and a feebler light shone from one of the upstairs windows.

She moved to the gate, opened it silently and slipped out. The rearseat window was open. Odd how the criminal never fancied that he might become a victim, she mused, shining her torch cautiously into the car.

It was littered with cigarette ends, sweet papers, a couple of gaudy magazines. Across one open page a ribbon lay, pulled from a dark plait – she could see a few black hairs caught in the knot. It was whitish in the light of the torch but she knew that in daylight it would be red and that she had last seen it on the head of Tabitha Lee.

FIFTEEN

There was a sickness in her throat that she swallowed convulsively, turning and gliding swiftly along the outer walls of the enclosure until she reached the main gates and could take to her heels and run up the drive.

The police car was parked at the steps and Sister Marie stood at the half-open door.

'The police arrived a couple of minutes ago!' the latter said. 'Mother David says to go straight to the parlour.'

Tapping on the parlour door she felt a tremor of anxiety. So much to tell and so little evidence to offer presented a formidable task.

The two officers rose as she went in.

'*Dominus vobiscum.*'

'*Et cum spiritu tuo.*'

The customary responses struck a familiar note in the strangeness.

'Mother David, the uniform—' she began.

'Our lot sound as if they're arriving now,' said Sergeant Petrie.

'Luther's guarding the evidence,' Sister Joan said.

'In that case Sister Martha had better go with you,' said Mother David. 'I believe she handles Luther best. He isn't happy when any members of the Force are around. Sister Joan, you'll be relieved to hear that Sister Gabrielle has taken no hurt from her escapade though why she chose to wander off in the first place is a mystery! And where exactly have you been?'

'Looking for Alice, Mother, but Padraic found her.'

'And you found the uniform?' Inspector Mill asked.

'I gave Sister Gabrielle into Sister Perpetua's care,' she said patiently, 'and then I went to put Alice on the leash. She was tugging at something on one of the refuse heaps. Luther wandered up while I was there and I told him to stand guard. Then I came here to tell Mother David and then I went out again because Alice had run off. She was almost run over by Padraic's lorry.'

'What on earth was Padraic Lee driving near the convent for at this time of night?' Mother David asked.

'Looking for Tabitha. She didn't go home after school – Alan, I mean Inspector Mill, that's something I have to tell you! One of Tabitha's red hair ribbons is on the back seat of the tenants' car. I've just seen it there!'

'You went to the old postulancy? Why?'

'I don't know, Mother David,' Sister Joan said lamely. 'I just had a feeling.'

Mother David twitched her nose, opened her mouth to speak, then discreetly closed it again.

'We'd better get over there,' Inspector Mill said. 'Not that a ribbon proves anything.'

'Sister Joan, perhaps you would show the gentlemen out?' Mother David said. 'Then we shall have a belated supper.'

'I'm afraid we are to blame,' the inspector began.

'Our duty as civilians must also rank as important,' Mother David said. '*Dominus vobiscum.*'

'*Et cum spiritu tuo.*'

Sister Joan led the way to the front steps.

'So Tabitha Lee's missing?' Inspector Mill paused to look at her. 'Any ideas?'

'I think she is – or at least was with the tenants,' she told him.

'And?'

'And I think the tenants are mixed up in everything that has gone on. I know they didn't arrive until after the earlier incidents but there's something about them – I'm sorry but—'

'We'll go and ask questions about hair ribbons,' he said.

In the kitchen Sister Marie was looking mournfully at a sad-looking cheese soufflé.

'It rose, fell and now just sits there,' she said.

'Like the Roman Empire,' Sister Joan told her. 'Come, I'll help you dish up.'

'Sister Perpetua is having hers in the infirmary with the old ladies,' Sister Marie told her. 'I do wonder why Sister Gabrielle decided to go for a walk.'

'Old ladies have their foibles,' Sister Joan told her.

A somewhat depleted party gathered in the refectory for a belated supper: it was Sister Katherine's turn to read aloud while the others supped.

For not the first time Sister Joan found her attention straying from the trials of the saint whose history was being read to more immediate concerns.

She could picture the quiet but relentless search of the garden. She could imagine the correct but probing questioning of the tenants. And always in her mind was the memory of Mrs Pearson, candles burning about her, eyes wide open and fixed on something too horrible to describe.

'Thank you, Sister Katherine. Enjoy your supper now.' Mother David folded her napkin carefully. 'I am half inclined to cancel recreation but perhaps it's better to return as quickly as possible to the normal routine. Sister Joan, will you go over to the garden and see the constabulary has everything it needs? And while you are about it check the customary locks.'

'Yes, Mother. Shall I take Alice?'

'I believe Alice has had quite enough excitement for one evening,' Mother David said.

Her mouth betrayed amusement.

Outside, full night had cloaked the enclosure in blackness only broken by the flare of torches as the police moved about their task. Tape marked the limits of the search area. A police photographer was taking pictures.

'They let you out after dark I see,' Inspector Mill commented as she hesitated.

'Have they found anything else?'

'The chopped up remains of a couple of wicker shopping baskets. Soaked with paraffin and ready for the burning. Oh, and Padraic rang the station to say that Tabitha turned up safe and well. She swears she was by herself in the amusement arcade. Apparently she'd arranged to meet some lad there and he never showed up. Padraic said she was sulky and evasive and not inclined to answer questions.'

'And the hair ribbon?'

She asked the question sharply as he stepped over the tape to stand beside her.

'No sign of it,' he said shortly.

'Alan, it was there on the rear seat of the car. I wasn't mistaken!'

'I'm sure you thought you saw it.'

'Thought? Alan, I did see it!'

'Without evidence. . . .' He shrugged.

'Tabitha was carrying a couple of wicker baskets when I saw her. She said she was going to the camp but she evidently changed direction. She said she was taking shopping home but Padraic told me he hadn't asked her to get any.'

'You think the uniform was in the bags? You don't think that Tabitha had anything to do with Constable Seldon's death, surely?'

'No, of course not! But she may have been persuaded to get rid of the stuff.'

'By your tenants? Sister, I questioned them. I can't say they're the most prepossessing group I ever met. The mother, Winifred Roye, is a bit of a battleaxe if I'm any judge and the daughters are pretty rough in their speech, and the son-in-law strikes me as a shifty little devil, but I've no cause to hold them for further questioning. The son-in-law's father is visiting for a week or so from Liverpool and there's a friend—'

'Henrico del Marco.'

'Well, I can run a check on his immigrant status but there's no reason to think any of the others had anything to do with anything. In any case they were up in Liverpool when the earlier incidents occurred. You can't hold people because they use the odd four-letter word.'

'I suppose not,' she said resignedly.

'However your evidence will now be needed at the inquest. I'm going to ask for a week's postponement in order to get full forensic details from the uniform and the baskets. I'll speak to Mother David.'

'Have you seen Luther?'

'He'll have rushed off to Brother Cuthbert's place or wherever he spends his nights.'

'And I must check the locks,' she said. 'Good night, Inspector.'

' 'Night, Sister.'

She lifted her hand and moved back towards the main house. It looked, she mused, as she paused briefly to survey it with only the light from her torch and the dimmed lights from one or two of the curtained windows illuminating its grey stone mass, like the abode of some wealthy family forever stuck in Victorian times.

Lilith nuzzled her when she reached the stable, hoping for a last titbit.

'I've a lump of sugar somewhere about me,' Sister Joan said, finding it in her pocket.

'Sister, is everything all right?'

Sister Dorothy hove into indistinct view.

'As right as it can be under the circumstances,' Sister Joan said moodily.

'You're letting the outside world affect you.' Sister Dorothy shook her head in reproof. 'That was always your problem, Sister. We are vowed to the religious life, not to helping solve crimes.'

191

'And there's no solving anything without evidence.'

'Never fear! Evil destroys itself in the end. It's almost time for prayers and blessing. Are the locks checked?'

'Only the stable and kitchen door.'

She tested the former as she left the stable with Lilith contentedly munching and began her circuit of the building. Sister Dorothy moving towards the kitchen said cheerfully, 'Stop fretting, Sister. Truth will out!'

But not for Mrs Pearson and not for Melanie Seldon, Sister Joan reflected, perhaps not for young Tabitha Lee either if she had allowed herself to be embroiled in anything.

As she rounded the last corner Mother David opened the front door.

'The locks are all checked—' Sister Joan began.

'I'm sure they are, Sister! It's come to a pretty pass when I have to send one of my nuns on sentry duty.' The prioress pushed up her spectacles and gave what in a larger woman might've been described as a faint bellow of indignation.

'Will we lock the chapel too?' Sister Joan asked as she fell into step beside her.

'The chapel here is never locked,' Mother David said. 'It stays open, as you know, for the comfort of any poor soul who strays by night across the moors. Oh!'

She had stopped short.

'Mother Prioress?'

'I have composed a short statement to cover the most recent events so that we can then put them aside and concentrate on prayer. I left it on my desk.'

'I'll get it for you. I can bolt the front door at the same time.'

'Two small sheets of paper in the top – no, I believe the second drawer down. I'll go on into chapel.'

She swept ahead, cloak billowing. Sister Joan went into the hall, drew the bolts firmly and went through to the parlour.

The parlour was shrouded in darkness. She moved to the desk and switched on the reading lamp there. The top drawer, Mother David had said, or maybe the second. For a prioress so recently elected she was not to be blamed in the light of current events if she occasionally got things a trifle muddled.

The top drawer held some prayer cards, two sheets of carefully written notes – evidently the notes referred to – and some letters marked Correspondence Answered. On top the letter of recommendation from Father John Fitzgerald had been neatly ticked.

For a long moment she stared at it, scanning the words of commendation, the backward slanting loops of the signature. Then as if of its own volition her hand moved to the telephone.

'Number please of a Father John Fitzgerald in Liverpool?' she requested.

'Do you have an address?'

'Yes, of course. One moment!'

She scanned the letter hastily.

'The Manse, Bristol Road.'

'There's no Fitzgerald at that address,' came the operator's voice a couple of moments later. 'There's a Manse in Fleming Street, a Father John Fitzgerald. Shall I give you that number?'

'Who lives at the first address I gave?' Sister Joan asked.

'I'm sorry. I'm not permitted to say,' the voice informed her. 'The number is coming up now.'

She grabbed a pencil and scribbled it down on the edge of the letter.

Dialling it she felt a tremor of unease. Then the receiver at the other end was lifted.

'Yes?'

A female voice. Sister Joan drew a breath and said steadily, 'This is Sister Joan from the Order of the Daughters of Compassion from our house in Cornwall. Is Father John Fitzgerald available. I apologize for the lateness of the hour.'

'I'm very sorry, Sister.' The voice had warmed slightly. 'This is his housekeeper, Mrs Doolley speaking. I'm afraid Father John is still away.'

'Away? I wasn't aware—'

'He went over to the United States in mid August,' Mrs Doolley informed her. 'A four-month sabbatical and a conference in Chicago to attend. We've had a succession of curates since so I'll be very pleased when he's home again. Would you like to leave a message?'

'No. No message,' Sister Joan said, and replaced the receiver with numb fingers.

So Father John Fitzgerald hadn't written the letter and he didn't live at the Manse in Bristol Road. He'd been away in America when the advertisement for tenants had been placed in the newspapers. Someone else had used his name and written the letter.

She lifted the receiver and dialled the original number that was neatly hand printed below the date on the letter itself.

A ringing tone ensued and then a male voice, 'Sorry, but I'm not here to take calls at the moment. If you want to leave your name and address I'll get back to you.'

She put the receiver down, folded up the letter and slipped it into her pocket, took up the handwritten notes for which Mother David had asked and closed the drawer.

In the chapel, the nuns already knelt, heads bowed, rosary beads dripping from their fingers.

Sister Joan moved forward to give Mother David the notes and sank to her knees in her usual place.

'We have now concluded the Sorrowful Mysteries' – a swiftly veiled but reproachful glance in Sister Joan's direction – 'and it seems to me appropriate,' Mother David said, 'that we should have concentrated on the sorrows of Our Blessed Lady since in recent weeks we have been much disturbed, as have others in this district, by events which, though not proven to be connected, have definitely borne the stamp of wrongdoing – even of evil. Alice was missing and found with a hurt paw tied on the quay side, Padraic Lee's dog was found poisoned; then a lady in the town, Mrs Pearson, died of an unexpected heart attack shortly after her pet cat had been found drowned – all, as I say, apparently unrelated but troubling. Most deeply troubling.'

She paused to take breath, her eyes behind the round spectacles lifted to the statue of the Madonna behind which the steps spiralled to the library. When she resumed her voice was firmer.

'And now a young policewoman has been found dead in the river, killed apparently by a blow on the head, her uniform taken and used, I am informed, by some person impersonating her in order to delay any investigation as to her whereabouts. That uniform has now been found in one of the bonfire heaps in the enclosure. The police have sectioned off that area of the garden so for the moment while their investigations are continuing that section is out of bounds. Sister Martha, you must make Luther aware of that.'

'Luther won't come near while there are police around,' Sister Martha said.

'Let us, each one of us, privately pray that the criminal or criminals responsible for the death of a young woman are apprehended and brought to justice. We have had a most upsetting day, not aided by the illness of our two priests. We must pray for their swift recovery. Sister Joan, in the morning I would like you to go down to the presbytery to enquire after them and find out from Sister Jerome if there is any help we can offer.'

'Yes, Mother Prioress,' Sister Joan nodded.

'Tomorrow there will be no Mass offered in this chapel but we will come down as usual and occupy that time in prayer. Sister Perpetua, will you make quite certain that none of our . . . more elderly sisters take it into their heads to go wandering?'

'Both are already tucked up,' Sister Perpetua said. 'Sister Gabrielle was more tired than she knew and Sister Mary Concepta – she does seem to be failing now that the winter's almost upon us.'

'You think a medical opinion is required?'

'Not at the moment, Mother David, but I shall keep a very

close eye on her,' Sister Perpetua said.

'As you always do, Sister. That seems to be all.' Mother David passed the sheets back to Sister Joan. 'As you know our house is locked after recreation every night. I have asked Sister Joan to double-check the locks and to ensure the stable is bolted. The chapel will remain open for any soul wishing to use it. Let us begin the final prayers. Our Father—'

On her knees with the rest, Sister Joan repeated the familiar words. She could hear Sister Perpetua's firm, rounded voice and the sweet whisper of Sister Katherine as they made the last petitions of the night before the grand silence.

Odd how even after years of joined prayer the voices still retained some spark of the individual natures of the sisters, she mused. The voice was one of the most recognizable features of any individual human being.

And somewhere while she had listened to that recorded voice on the answering machine – somewhere she had heard that voice before.

SIXTEEN

'Father Malone is still a mite chesty,' Sister Jerome said, opening the door to Sister Joan and looking relieved to see the van instead of Lilith parked outside the presbytery gate. 'Father Stephen is almost his old self again. He offered Mass this morning and would've come up to the convent but I put my foot down.'

'Very sensible of you, Sister,' Sister Joan said with a touch of amusement.

She doubted if she would ever see the day when any priest would stand up to the housekeeper's maternal bullying.

'Sister Marie sent some pears over and the last lot of black-berries she froze.'

She handed over the gifts.

'That was kind of her! At this end of the year fruit is always so expensive. I'm afraid I persuaded Father Malone to have an extra day in his room but if you want to see Father Stephen I can bring you a cup of tea,' Sister Jerome said. 'Go into the study, Sister.'

'Father Stephen is just the person I want to see,' Sister Joan said with satisfaction.

In the study where a fire blazed on the hearth a somewhat pale Father Stephen rose to greet her.

'Are all well up at the convent, Sister?' He indicated a chair and resumed his own. 'We have heard most disturbing reports about events in the town.'

'Yes. Constable Seldon seems definitely to have been murdered,' Sister Joan told him. 'Father Stephen, I need to know something.'

'Yes?' He broke off as Sister Jerome bustled in with two cups of tea and bustled out again, closing the door behind her with heroic self-control.

'Your handwriting. . . .' She hesitated.

'You find it difficult to read?'

'No. In fact I've seen very few examples of it,' she admitted. 'I did wonder – those backward loops—'

'Ornate, aren't they?' He gave a sudden boyish grin. 'Blame my Latin master for that! Father Fitzgerald had a passion for the medieval style. He insisted that all his pupils adapted their writing to suit what he called the decorative glory of the Gothic!'

'Father John Fitzgerald?' she asked sharply.

'And still going strong. I understand from Mother David that he recommended your present tenants.'

'You went to school in Liverpool?'

For no good reason she had pictured him in some exclusive boys' public school.

'I haven't been back there for years. Haven't seen Father Fitzgerald for years either,' he ruminated.

'Father Stephen, when you were at school did you know a pupil named Lurgan – Ian Lurgan?'

'What year?'

'He'd be about thirty now.'

'Then he'd've been in the first stream and I'd've been lower sixth. I can't say the name means anything.'

'But it would be possible to get a list of old pupils for those years?'

'I suppose one could. You have some particular reason?' he began.

'Yes. I have a particular reason. Thank you, Father. I'd better be getting back.'

'Lurgan.' Chin on hand he stared into the blazing fire. 'Wait a moment – there was a Lurgan – can't recall his first name or what he looked like – but the name itself does ring a bell. Not a common name.'

'What do you recall about it?' she asked.

'Not Catholics but the boy got a place at the school on – ah yes, compassionate grounds. Mother committed suicide. I think that was it. I seem to remember also that he didn't stay long. Discipline problems.'

'Thank you, Father.'

'One hopes,' he said, 'that this recent tragedy will soon be cleared up.'

'Yes indeed – no, please don't get up, Father! I am glad to find you so much better. I can see myself out.'

At the door she paused abruptly, another question spilling from her lips.

'The boy's mother – the one who committed suicide. Would you recall where she came from?'

'Somewhere in Plymouth I believe. I think she was buried there. Is it important?'

'It might be,' Sister Joan said, grimly, and closed the door behind her.

Ten minutes later she was in the police station, refusing a cup of coffee, Inspector Mill seated opposite her.

'It's early days for any further forensic evidence,' he said. 'I can tell you that the uniform was definitely Constable Seldon's. It's been ripped and torn and soaked in paraffin but of course if whoever wore it to impersonate her shed a drop of sweat or even a hair – then we might have something. But whoever carried this out is very clever and very cunning. They'll have worn gloves throughout. However we can but hope.'

'Perhaps more than that!' Swiftly she related the information she had received from Father Stephen.

'That can't be the only school in the country that favours Gothic script,' he objected.

'But not with such distinctive back slanting loops,' she pressed.

199

'So you say Father John Fitzgerald was away when the recommendation he supposedly wrote arrived at the convent.'

'From the wrong address,' she reminded him. 'If you checked out the address we had – Mother David never did – one expects a letter from a priest to be written by a priest from his presbytery. If you checked out that address you'd almost certainly find that a Mr Timothy Lurgan was living there until recently.'

'Proving what? That he falsified a reference for his son and in-laws so they could move into the old postulancy? We'd never get it into court with the recent crime rates rising.'

'And Mrs Lurgan who killed herself came from Plymouth and—'

'And Melanie Seldon's young brother killed himself in Plymouth. And Plymouth is a big city.'

'The son, Ian Lurgan, could have married a girl from Plymouth. The Royes might come from Plymouth. They could've have moved down there a few years back after Mrs Lurgan killed herself.'

'Leaving Tim Lurgan up in Liverpool to wait several years until Melanie Seldon's brother had killed himself and she'd trained to be a police officer and then they join up together and come down into Cornwall to kill her. Sister, for once you're not making sense! Oh, I'll grant you that Tim Lurgan probably remained in Liverpool and, as a favour to his son's in-laws, faked a letter from Father Fitzgerald.'

'They said they'd just moved from Liverpool. I believe they've been living in Plymouth since before the Seldon boy's suicide.'

'You met them at the station,' he reminded her.

'They were already waiting on the platform when I got to the station.'

'Having just travelled from Plymouth instead of Liverpool. It isn't a crime to say you've just arrived from one place when in reality you've just arrived from another.'

'But you could find out.'

'Yes I could but it wouldn't prove anything illegal at all. And I've a budget to stick to!'

'Oh budgets!' she said impatiently.

'Yes, budgets – and if they've actually been in Plymouth, with Tim Lurgan still up in Liverpool there's no way of tracing them easily. They could have been moving from one cheap rental to another.'

'The Benefits Agency—'

'Has its hands full with false claims and asylum seekers. And if they have been in Plymouth,' he said, 'then there's no connection between Mrs Pearson's seeing devils in church-yards or the poisoning of Padraic Lee's dog or the drowning of the cat or—'

'Or Alice being lured away. I know. But Plymouth is hardly the other end of the country and the sister, Kit Roye, does have a car.'

'But why go to all the trouble to come here?' he demanded. 'Both Liverpool and Plymouth must contain plenty of dogs and cats and elderly ladies with a belief in the occult. Why come to this town at all?'

'I don't know!' She shrugged helplessly as she rose. 'Alan, are you telling me that there's nothing we can do?'

'At present – not a thing.'

'If they were in Plymouth and caused the Seldon boy to kill himself then perhaps Melanie Seldon suspected them and couldn't do anything about it at the time,' she suggested. 'She decided to join the Force and when she heard they were coming here she applied for a transfer—'

'How would she know that?'

'Maybe she knew them casually, kept tabs on them—'

'There were no notes anywhere in her bedsit,' he said.

'They'd've destroyed them once they got in, wouldn't they?'

'All supposition. Meanwhile we'll plod on with forensics.'

'And Tabitha Lee's hair ribbon? I did see it on the back seat of Kit's car. I did!'

'Nothing there when we looked. Sister, there's no evidence.'

201

'I'll find some!' she said. 'I swear I will.'

'I hope you do,' he said sombrely. 'I hope you do.'

There was still time before luncheon for her to spend an extra half-hour in town. On impulse she stopped at a florist's and bought some bronze dahlias, laying them on the seat beside her and driving to the cemetery.

The day had greyed and chilled, one last migrating bird uttering a doleful farewell as it headed south, the wind crisping the petals of the flowers as she carried them to the newly made grave.

There were others laid there – roses now shrivelled with a card signed by Melanie's mother, the police tribute of poppies and laurel, the flowers from the convent and a few anonymous bunches placed there by sympathetic townspeople. The plain wooden cross bore the name and rank, dates of birth and death. She supposed that Melanie's mother would come down when the stone was erected and carved.

Laying down the dahlias she felt the pricking of tears behind her eyelids. She hadn't taken to Constable Seldon and that somehow made it worse. For a friend she would surely have grieved more, made more effort to bring the killer to book.

The soft scrape of a shoe on the gravel made her turn abruptly. Henrico del Marco's broad shape blotted the sky.

'It's Sister Joan, isn't it? From the convent?'

His light curiously unaccented voice chilled her. She found herself taking a step backwards.

'Yes,' she said curtly.

'Pity about the young lady. It's a wicked world, Sister.'

'In many ways, yes,' she said.

'And an old lady died here too just before we arrived. A heart attack, wasn't it?'

'Yes. A sudden heart attack.'

'I thought I'd come down and have a walk around,' he said. 'I like graveyards – peaceful places.'

'Usually,' she said.

'Not usually places where devils lurk.'

'How did—?'

'Just an expression, Sister!' He shot her an amused glance. 'Did you know the young lady well?'

'Hardly at all,' Sister Joan said coldly.

'Then how kind of you to bring extra flowers!'

'I happened to be in the vicinity,' she hedged. 'If you'll excuse me I have to get back for lunch.'

'Ah yes, the rules. We are all bound by rules, by promises and vows. You know this town is a pleasant place, even at this season. I may stay on for a few weeks.'

'I would have thought that Italy would be warmer in the winter,' she said.

'Ah, yes, but on the mountains there is always snow.'

'And the tenants are not permitted to sublet the property.'

'But permitted to entertain guests, I believe. It's been nice talking to you, Sister. I'm on my way up to the school.'

'The school?' She hadn't meant to question but his remark took her by surprise.

'I like to watch young people,' he said. 'One recaptures one's own youth in watching them.'

'In this country middle-aged men who hang round schools are apt to be regarded with suspicion,' she said.

'Ah, nothing like that, Sister!' He gave a low chuckle that grated along her nerves. 'Oh, dear me, no! The corruption of the body will take place over years – Nature sees to that! – but the corruption of minds is altogether more exciting. I speak theoretically, of course.'

'I'm sure you do,' Sister Joan said. 'Good day to you, Mr del Marco.'

She feared he would keep in step with her but he turned and walked away rapidly.

A familiar tonsured figure stood by the van.

'Brother Cuthbert! What are you doing in town?' she enquired.

'I walked down to ask after Father Malone and Father Stephen.' The usual smile was missing from his face as he stared after the retreating figure.

'That was Henrico del Marco,' Sister Joan said. 'He's staying with the tenants.'

'An Italian?'

'I'm not sure where he comes from or even if he's supposed to be in this country.'

'One finds del Marcos in every country,' Brother Cuthbert said thoughtfully. 'Leeches, hangers-on. Not important in themselves but a trap for unwary youth. Odd but they don't usually stay when I'm around. One would like to know what motivates them, how best to combat it. Well, he's not of great importance.'

'Would you like a lift back?'

'I would indeed, Sister! That's most kind of you!'

Something of his usual joviality had returned. He held open the van door for her to enter and then went round to the passenger seat.

'I called at the presbytery,' she volunteered, letting in the clutch. 'The invalids seem much improved.'

'Thank God they do! And Sister Jerome is an excellent housekeeper. A real Saint Martha.'

'Whom Christ rebuked,' she reminded him.

'Is that how you read the passage, Sister? Now I glean a very different idea which may not be entirely valid but then I never was a theologian. I think Our Lord was teasing Saint Martha, joshing her a little bit.'

'Joshing her?' she echoed.

'Or whatever the Aramaic expression might be! You know, in the style of "Come on, Martha, we know you're proud of your cooking but ease up a little". You know?'

'It doesn't say anywhere that Our Lord laughed,' she said.

'They probably forgot to mention it. And there is no weapon stronger than laughter against the Devil. I think we must encourage more laughter,' he said thoughtfully.

' "The Devil hateth a mocking spirit",' she quoted slowly. 'Do you honestly sense devilry about, Brother Cuthbert?'

'Oh, he's generally around but when he finds disciples – we must try to keep very cheerful, Sister.'

'Right! More mirth is requested,' she said, and drove briskly on to the side track that meandered over the hill.

'Thanks for the lift. Lazy of me but I seem to be behindhand in my work,' he said, as she drew up outside the old school-house.

'You've supplied us with plenty of wood.'

'Not that sort of work,' he said with a slight smile. 'Good day to you, Sister Joan. Try not to fret.'

'I'm hoping there will be an end to all this unpleasantness soon,' she said impatiently.

'There's always an end to it,' Brother Cuthbert said and went, whistling, into his lodging.

At the kitchen door she drew up in time to see Padraic emerge.

'Sister Marie was kind enough to make me a sandwich,' he said, opening the van door and helping her down with some ceremony. 'You know she reminds me of Sister Teresa more and more every day.'

'We had a letter from her last week,' she remembered to tell him. 'Her father is still very ill, I fear. Still one can always hope. Is Tabitha—?'

'Secret as the grave,' he said ruefully. 'The police came over and asked her if she'd been with the Lurgans or in their car. She said she hadn't. Went on saying it even after the police left. I felt like giving her a good beating but I've never hit my girls and I don't reckon on starting down that road now. But there's summat she's not telling.'

'Have you spoken to our tenants?' she asked.

He shook his head. 'I keep well clear but I had a word with the school, told them to keep an eye on her and I told Tabitha she doesn't hang about the arcade after school hours any longer.'

'What did she say?'

'She laughed,' he said, his tone uneasy and puzzled. 'She

just laughed and then she said, "If it was only that," and clammed up like an oyster.'

'If it was only that,' Sister Joan repeated. 'I'll try to make sense of it, Padraic. Give the girls my love.'

'I will that, Sister. Kushti, heel!'

He walked off, leaving her to go into the kitchen where Sister Marie was contemplating half-a-dozen fresh trout with a mixture of delight and embarrassment.

'He's always so kind,' she said, 'but all this fish and no payment ever accepted.'

'Have them poached, Sister Marie!' Sister Joan said on a spurt of unexpected mirth.

'In time for lunch!' Sister Gabrielle, stomping across the hall, greeted her with a snort.

'For a wonder,' Sister Joan agreed. 'And you're none the worse?'

'Not at all. The walk did me good,' Sister Gabrielle said.

'Sister Gabrielle, why did you walk in that direction?' Sister Joan asked. 'Towards the old postulancy? Why so far? Was there something – someone you needed to check on?'

For an instant the old eyes flickered. Then Sister Gabrielle said harshly, 'You ask too many questions, Sister!'

She turned and stomped on, every tap of her walking stick an indignant exclamation as she moved across the hall.

Do I? Do I spend so much time ferreting out things that I neglect my more important spiritual duties?

The problem nagged at her as she turned towards the chapel. The inner door, leading past the small parlours for visitors and sisters, opened into the side wall just before the Lady Altar. Sister Hilaria was on her knees in her usual pew and a scent of rosewater perfumed the air.

'Sister Joan?' Sister Dorothy, descending from the library, nodded to her as she reached ground level.

'Yes, Sister?'

'Would you be kind enough to bring down the list of menus on my desk? Sister Marie has taken it into her head to have menus for feast days and with All Saints so close.'

'I'll get them for you, Sister.'

She dipped into a genuflection and went up the winding stairs.

The light had been switched off but daylight filtered through the narrow windows on to the shelves, the cabinets in which documents and booklets were stored, the desk with its neatly printed menus.

Was Sister Marie planning on serving roast salmon, lobster thermidor and strawberry soufflé out of season, she wondered, amused as she picked up the neatly typed lists?

Downstairs the dinner gong, brought into action at lunchtimes too, reverberated.

The door leading to the two storerooms was closed. A little light and air there wouldn't come amiss, she decided, reminding herself that it was days since she'd carted a broom up here to sweep away the dust that gathered in the crevices between the bare boards.

The drawings and sketches for Mother David's *Lives of the Saints* were pinned neatly on a cardboard frame. Had been pinned.

She stood, staring at the empty frame. Had Mother David taken them downstairs to the parlour? It would've been unlike her to touch them without consulting her.

At her feet, as she involuntarily glanced down, the mark of a print showed clearly in a patch of dust. A cloven footprint, she saw, and felt panic invade her.

SEVENTEEN

'All the drawings gone, Sister? You're certain?' Mother David gazed at her intently from the other side of the desk.

'All gone,' Sister Joan said tonelessly. 'I asked Sister Dorothy if she'd seen them recently but she hasn't. She wouldn't have touched them anyway. Nobody here would.'

'I thought you ate very little at lunchtime,' Mother David said.

'And you've seen the footprint? Drawn in black chalk and not a genuine print at all.'

'To show us that the evil is here inside this house. But when could it have been—?'

'Any time after the grand silence,' Sister Joan said. 'The chapel stays open; only the inner door to our quarters is bolted, and the door to the library is fastened but the storerooms are never locked. Anyone might sneak in and take them.'

'Will you inform the police? You have my leave.'

'To what purpose?' Sister Joan made a defeated gesture. 'The drawings weren't valuable. I can do them again and I will. At the most it would be trespass and petty theft. You may be sure there will be no other prints! There were none except my own at Mrs Pearson's cottage nor in the bedsit where Constable Seldon died. There will be no trace on the uniform buried in the garden rubble. If there are any prints on the broken pieces of basket they will only be Tabitha's prints and

209

I am certain that she has no idea what she is getting herself into.'

'We could evict the tenants. The letter of recommendation was a forgery.'

'Would that be sufficient grounds?' Sister Joan wondered. 'I think you will probably find that Tim Lurgan, Ian Lurgan's father, was a fairly regular communicant up in Liverpool, that he got hold of a sample of Father John Fitzgerald's very individual signature and traced it at the bottom of the letter he sent. The rest of it was typed. And even when Father Fitzgerald returns to his parish – he must write dozens and dozens of letters – so how could he recall one as not being genuine? He's getting on in years.'

'And Ian Lurgan was his pupil you said?'

'Father Stephen had some recollections of him as a much younger pupil at the same school. Tim Lurgan's wife came from Plymouth and killed herself when Ian was a child. They were living in Liverpool then, I suspect. Later on they moved down to Plymouth where Constable Seldon's half-brother killed himself. My guess is that Tim Lurgan returned to Liverpool and the rest of them moved nearer this town, evading any questioning, planning their next move.'

'And Constable Seldon followed them? Sister, this sounds like the wildest guesswork!'

'With no concrete evidence. I know. But, Mother David, when they left Plymouth they would have lain low for a while, separated, maybe a couple of them came down here to look round the town, to start the mischief working here.'

'And killed Constable Seldon because she knew about them? Sister Joan, without solid proof there's nothing to connect them to anything,' Mother David said impatiently. 'I am not, thank heavens, a police officer but don't crimes require motive, means and opportunity? Where's the motive?'

'Love of evil?'

'And that, my dear girl, won't stand up in a court of law any more than love of good entitles us to be canonized!'

'I know,' Sister Joan said.

'I will look very closely at the contract for the tenancy in case they are in breach of any of the rules,' the prioress said. 'As it is, the fact that in some ways they seem to be somewhat unsuitable tenants doesn't entitle us to mount a witch hunt. All men are innocent until proved guilty.'

Presumed innocent, Sister Joan thought, but didn't say. Aloud she said. 'You don't wish this latest act to be made known to the community?'

'I think it's best kept to ourselves, Sister,' Mother David said. 'Next week we renew our vows and prepare for All Saints' Day; Sister Mary Concepta is in very far from robust health and our serenity of mind has already been disturbed quite enough by the visit from the police and the search of the gardens. When Father John Fitzgerald returns to his parish I will make some discreet enquiries of him. Thank you, Sister.' *Dominus vobiscum.*'

'*Et cum spiritu tuo,*' Sister Joan said, rising from her stool.

Going into the hall, Sister Joan carefully unclenched her fists. Common sense told her that Mother David's point of view was both logical and reasonable, that a case was nothing without strong evidence, that one's personal prejudices had to be overridden. Every nerve in her system told another tale.

Sister Perpetua, looking harassed, came out of the infirmary.

'Are you going into town for anything, Sister?' she enquired.

'What did you want, Sister?'

'Sister Mary Concepta's prescription needs to be collected. She is really very far from well. If this continues—'

'I'll get it for you at once,' Sister Joan said.

'No need to break your neck over it,' Sister Perpetua said, with a sniff. 'We have enough tablets for a couple of days but one likes to have a good supply.'

'I could take Sister Gabrielle for a spin,' Sister Joan said with a flash of mischief.

'Would that you could, Sister!' The infirmarian gave a faint grin. 'But quite honestly one couldn't wean her from Sister Mary Concepta's bedside save for a Papal Decree. They both came originally from the same village in Ireland. Did you know that?'

'No, I didn't.'

'Well, we're not supposed to chat about our former lives anyway, but Sister Mary Concepta let it slip in conversation recently. She was reminding Sister Gabrielle that the latter used to have red hair and could dance at the ceilidhs more skilfully than any other in the village.'

'I'll get the prescription,' Sister Joan said.

She called Alice who leapt up into the van and devoted several moments to making herself comfortable in the rear, started the engine and drove down into the town.

Her heart felt heavy as if a weight had settled upon it. The case of Melanie Seldon seemed to be proceeding at an unusually slow rate; Sister Mary Concepta was obviously failing which would be a particular grief for Sister Gabrielle despite their occasional squabbles, and the theft of the drawings, while personally annoying, was the more serious in that it proved the perpetrators of the various events were becoming bolder.

The prescription being duly presented and filled, she climbed back into the van just as an unwelcome figure hove into view.

'Sister Joan, are you driving back to the convent?'

'Yes I am, Mr Lurgan.'

'I don't suppose—?' He tilted his head to one side and glanced at her out of his long, light, curiously flat pupilled eyes. 'I don't suppose you could give me a lift back? My dad and Dawn have gone off somewhere together and I didn't bring any change for the next bus.'

'I suppose so,' she said curtly, not liking it much when he climbed up into the passenger seat beside her.

In the rear of the van Alice growled, softly and unexpectedly.

'I hear things aren't too good at the convent,' was his next remark.

'Then you hear wrongly, Mr Lurgan. Life proceeds at its usual rate.'

'But losing your drawings must've been a shock for you,' he said softly.

'What?' The word was jerked out of her as she swerved on to the side road.

'The drawings you were doing,' he said. 'All taken. What a pity!'

'Who told you about them?' she demanded.

'Well now, I can't rightly say. Be breaking a confidence. I can guess who took them though. Those gyppos—'

'Wouldn't dream of such a thing.'

'Bad blood,' he said musingly. 'Do you believe in bad blood?'

'No, I don't. If you don't mind, Mr Lurgan, I need to concentrate on my driving.'

'Yes. Now I don't like driving. Too nervous by far, and Dawn doesn't help you know. Always telling me what an idiot I am. To be honest, Sister, I'd like to get away from the whole crowd—'

'Mr Lurgan!' She brought the van to a shuddering halt. 'For the last time will you stop trying to drag me into your affairs? They are none of my business. I am unable to help you and I'm really not interested. If you don't approve of the actions of your wife and relatives then you should leave her and get yourself a decent job.'

'Oh, I will one day, Sister.' He had opened the rear seat door and was twisting himself about. 'Shall I take Alice for a nice run for you? I'm very fond of animals you know.'

'I would prefer you to get out and walk the rest of the way,' she said stonily. 'Close the rear door if you please. Alice isn't going anywhere with you!'

'Right you are!' Obeying he slid down to the ground, a spark of something in his eyes almost impossible to define.

213

'If you feel uneasy,' she said on impulse, 'leave them. Talk to Brother Cuthbert or to one of the priests. You don't have to—'

'Oh, but I do, Sister.' The spark had fled and the light eyes were alien again. 'There's Samhain still to come.'

'Sam what?'

She spoke to the air as he ducked and dived away, capering over the grassy mounds that marked the beginning of the moors.

Shiveringly she closed the door and drove on up to the school.

'Sister Joan, are you all right?'

Brother Cuthbert, just emerging from the door, stopped to stare as she slewed to a halt.

'Brother Cuthbert, what is Samhain?' she asked.

'Samhain? Why, it's All Hallows' Eve,' he said promptly. 'October the thirty-first.'

'Halloween?'

'The night when those vowed to the dark renew their vows. The dark side of the beginning of All Saints' Day. Why do you want to—? Oh, I see!'

He looked past her towards the capering figure diminishing into the distance.

'He as good as told me,' she said. 'He as good as told me.'

'I feared something like this.' Brother Cuthbert shook his head slightly. 'It goes on you know, all over the world. Evil for evil's sake. And seldom any proof of anything. Only straws in the wind.'

'Mrs Pearson?'

'A harmless old lady who knew a little but not enough to protect herself. Every coin has two sides, Sister.'

'But what are you going to do?'

'Pray and leave the rest to Heaven,' he said simply.

'In this day and age who would credit it?' she said slowly.

'In every day and age, Sister, evil creeps in. In every town, every village, like some deadly virus that poisons all it touches.

The same fight since the beginning of time. Don't imagine for one moment that anyone is immune and don't imagine either that anyone is incapable of fighting it.'

He touched her shoulder briefly like comrades at the start of a battle, turned and walked away.

She drove on slowly to the convent. There were two cars parked at the gates and Sister Dorothy hurried to meet her.

'Sister Mary Concepta took a turn for the worse,' she said. 'Father Stephen and the doctor are with her now. She is drifting away from us.'

'Sister Gabrielle?'

'She went into chapel for a while. I think she went out into the garden.'

'I'll find her,' Sister Joan said.

She found her within a few minutes, seated on a bench near one of the apple trees, prodding the ground with her stick.

'Ah, here you are, Sister!' She spoke brightly as Sister Joan sat down beside her.

'Aren't you cold out here?' Sister Joan said.

'A bit of fresh air blows the cobwebs away,' Sister Gabrielle said. 'You've heard about Mary Concepta? Well, there'll be a welcome waiting for her, that's certain! And what have you been up to? Still solving crimes?'

'Sister Gabrielle, can't you tell me why you were checking census lists and why you went over to the old postulancy?' Sister Joan asked.

There was such a long silence that she feared there would be no answer. Then Sister Gabrielle said, 'Between you and me, Sister, with no other person ever to be told?'

'You have my word.'

'Long ago back in Ireland,' Sister Gabrielle said, 'a lively young girl who loved dancing, a man with a smooth tongue. She dared not tell her family, so she came to England to work. She came to Liverpool. There was a daughter born. Winifred. Taken away shortly after birth of course. In those days girls didn't go getting pregnant and then running to the State for

215

help. And then, recently, in a peaceful little town in Cornwall odd, spiteful nastinesses began to happen. And then the tenants came.'

'Winifred Roye,' Sister Joan breathed.

'Imagine,' Sister Gabrielle said slowly, 'that a child fostered from birth grows up with a deep-seated hatred of the whole world. She blames the mother she never knew and one day, having been schooled in wickedness, for those of like mind always cluster together, she traces her.'

'From Liverpool to Plymouth and then to here?'

'The internet has many uses and not all of them are good,' the other said. 'She wants to make her presence felt, to disturb the tranquillity the mother forced to give her away has found, but she practises first, gains adherents to her cause. I went over to the old postulancy to see if I could catch one glimpse, some feature that was recognizable. I saw nothing but I was still certain.'

'In what year was Winifred Roye born?'

'In 1931. I entered the religious life a year later.'

'So you were twenty-two when – could you not have come to England at that age and kept the child?'

'Not me, Sister.' Sister Gabrielle briefly covered her companion's hand with her own. 'I was always more worldly wise than to believe the smooth flatteries of any man. Mary Concepta was only seventeen at that time. We have been talking of Sister Mary Concepta.'

'Who doesn't—?'

'Who doesn't know.' Sister Gabrielle said.

'Doesn't know anything?'

'Of recent events very little. And I have been careful that nothing has been said to her that might disturb her last weeks with us,' Sister Gabrielle said. 'You are the only person I have told. Keep it to yourself, Sister. We all have our little secrets.'

She patted Sister Joan's hand again and rose, leaning on her stick.

'Friendship,' Sister Joan whispered, 'is a truly holy thing.'

But evil couldn't be allowed to run on unchecked.

She rose from the bench and walked purposefully towards the old postulancy, her mouth set in a determined line.

They were all there, framed in the undrawn curtains of the living-room cum kitchen. Seated about the table with the remains of some kind of snack before them. Winifred Roye overflowed from her chair at the head of the table, round smooth face impassive, head turning slightly from side to side where her daughters sat – Dawn on the knees of Henrico del Marco, Kit with the red hair dyed a frowsty blonde and Tim Lurgan leaning over the back of her chair, eyes cast downwards. Ian Lurgan came into view and shot a startled glance towards the window.

The front door was ajar. She steeled her nerve and pushed it wider, turned to the right and stood, regarding them gravely.

'Well, this is a pleasant surprise,' Tim Lurgan began.

'You have a slight lisp in your speech,' she said coolly. 'I heard that same lisp before when I rang Liverpool. The telephone companies keep records so a voice trace wouldn't be hard to make. And a little further searching will bring to light exactly what drove your late wife to suicide. Your son's name will be on the registers of the school where elaborate Gothic writing was taught and encouraged, and it won't take long to find the silver mask with the horns and the black leotard in which your son enjoys frightening old ladies.'

'I don't know what the fuck you're on about,' Kit said.

'Oh, but you all do,' Sister Joan said. 'It took years to gather together your little group, didn't it? Many years of mischief making, of spitefulness and lewdness and dishonesty until you were ready to prove your worth. At Samhain would that be?'

'Ian, have you been babbling again?' Dawn turned a fierce gaze upon him.

'Honestly, babe! I never said a word!' he protested.

'The forensic tests will show that Tabitha Lee was in your car and she took the uniform in the baskets – did you leave it somewhere in town in case this building was searched? How

217

did you get her to comply? The promise of joining a secret society such as Melanie Seldon's young half-brother was persuaded to join? When I tell Padraic Lee—'

'What can he do?' Kit asked insolently.

'The Romanies have their methods and the police have theirs,' she said steadily, heart thudding. 'You're caught between the two and the master you are vowed to serve has no patience with mistakes. I merely came to tell you that time ran out.'

And pray God there is some forensic evidence, she thought as she backed slowly out of the room and through the front door.

When she was out of sight of the building she took to her heels and ran, veil flying out behind her. At the wildest edge of her imagining she could fancy cloven feet following her but when she glanced back she saw only the quiet graves in the little cemetery and Alice bounding to meet her.

EIGHTEEN

'I'm very sorry to hear about Sister Mary Concepta,' Inspector Mill said, pulling out a chair for her to sit upon.

'Thank you.' She seated herself. 'She was always rather delicate – in fact it's a miracle her heart lasted as long as it did. But she died very peacefully like a beautiful candle going out. The requiem will be a private one.'

'No family?'

'None known,' she said levelly. 'Inspector, you asked me to come down to the station—?'

'In view of Sister Mary Concepta's death I thought it wiser not to clutter up the convent with police activity,' he said.

'But you have the forensic results?'

'Nothing conclusive.'

'Oh, but surely—?'

'Whoever killed Constable Seldon for whatever reason left no prints and no DNA traces. Any they might have left were destroyed by the part burning of the uniform and its being soaked in paraffin. The two broken wicker baskets were equally unrewarding.'

'So we'll never be sure what happened?'

'We have done a little digging in other quarters. Timothy Lurgan, born in Liverpool in 1942, a bit of a drifter from the little we've been able to discover, married a local girl in 1966, – I say local but her grandparents lived in Plymouth. She took an overdose shortly after her son, Ian Lurgan, started school.

219

He and his father seemed to have drifted about from one lodging to another. Then, six years ago, they returned to Plymouth. Ian Lurgan married Dawn Roye in '92.'

'The Royes?'

'Winifred Roye, brought up in various foster homes, married a Fred Roye in '66 – her surname before that seems to have been changed every time she went to a new foster home. Her husband Fred was a welder by trade – inclined to take one drink too many – Dawn's the elder of their two daughters, Kit's the younger. The husband Fred died of alcoholic poisoning early last year.'

'Were they connected with Melanie Seldon's half-brother?'

'The younger girl, Kit, hung out at the same places and the two girls received cautions for shoplifting and dealing cannabis. Anyway neither girl held down any job for very long and Ian Lurgan has been living on benefits since he learned how to swindle the system. They all stuck together though, went up to Liverpool several times to stay with Timothy Lurgan. An expert would certainly be able to testify that he wrote the letter of recommendation pretending to be Father John Fitzgerald. He attended the same school his son later attended but never made much of an impression there. Then, while they were in Plymouth, Henrico del Marco turned up on the scene – that's not his real name by the way.'

'He's not Italian?'

'Henry Halton,' Inspector Mill said with a faint grin. 'Years back he was training for the priesthood.'

'What!'

'Got flung out of the seminary when he was caught offering up incense to the Devil. Joined a couple of rather suspect occult groups after that – did time for stalking young girls – reinvented himself as a man from Italy and met up with the Royes. Been a family friend ever since. Quite a motley crew, don't you think?'

'There must be something—' she began.

'Nothing that would stand up in court. It's not illegal to

change your name, hardly a hanging offence even to forge a letter of recommendation. It's my belief, though there's no evidence, that they found Plymouth too hot to hang around in, heard of the vacancy at your postulancy and came down here to quietly disappear for a while. Unfortunately, Melanie Seldon was on their track. She got herself posted here and foolishly decided to do some investigating on her own. Looking for hard evidence – who knows? I think she probably put on a dark cape and went over to the postulancy to see what she could find out.'

'And blinded me with a torch as she climbed over the wall.'

'And it's a fair bet that whoever was in that building at the time spotted her and decided she was getting too close for comfort.'

'And murdered her.'

'Whether accidentally or otherwise, we'll never know. The hiding of a body and the subsequent impersonation of a police officer are serious offences but without definite forensic evidence—'

'And one of them dressed up as a devil while they were visiting this area – Ian Lurgan?'

'Probably. Any occasion for a nasty practical joke. It was Mrs Pearson's ill fortune that she was tidying up the graveyard that night. I think that the so-called devil followed her home and decided to carry on tormenting her.'

'She brought protective candles to the postulancy.'

'Probably because you listened to her story and believed her. The Royes had already been busy in their small ways, of course – nicking the documents from the church vestry—'

'Sacristy, Inspector.'

'Whatever you call it. And the spoiled books in the postulancy which—'

'I got rid of,' she said.

'The poisoned lurcher, the drowned cat, luring Alice away—'

'They didn't kill Alice.'

'Maybe they were interrupted. Who knows? As it is,' he said

gloomily, 'all that I've told you is pure speculation. Nothing more. If I tried to get any of that on a charge sheet I'd be laughed out of court.'

'I drove past the postulancy on my way here,' she said. 'The car Kit Roye drove wasn't parked there and the curtains were all drawn.'

'Maybe they've all left town?'

'One wouldn't wish them on anybody else,' Sister Joan said.

'Well, sooner or later they'll probably come to grief. Will you give condolences to the prioress and the sisters. I only glimpsed Sister Mary Concepta once or twice but she looked like a sweet old lady.'

'Yes,' Sister Joan said. 'Yes, she was.'

'Of course they paid no rent,' Mother David said, her tone one of the deepest distaste. 'I ought to have specified a month at least in advance.'

'And the poor dear place was in an awful mess,' Sister Marie said. 'Spills and stains and – I'd hate to tell you what the toilets looked like.'

'Leave it to our imaginations!' Sister Dorothy begged.

'And that money was destined partly for the Order and partly for children's charities,' Sister Katherine mourned gently.

'Luther is going to help Sister Marie and me to clean the place up,' Sister Martha announced brightly.

'Shall we get on with our final discussion on the renewing of our vows?'

Mother David tapped the table with her pencil.

Extract from the *Liverpool Echo*, 31 October.

A horrific car crash held up traffic in the Mersey Tunnel for nearly two hours last night. A sports car with a young woman at the wheel sped out of control and overturned, bursting into flames. The car itself appeared to have

contained, apart from the driver, two females, one
elderly, and two males, one elderly. Formal identification
is now being sought. The remains of the victims were
taken to a nearby hospital but have not, so far, been identified.

Extract from a local newspaper, Aberdeen.

Learn to unlock the magic of your personality. Learn the
secrets of Ancient Egypt, secrets the Christian churches
tried to hide for ever. Have fun with the Dark Forces.
Apply to Harry Marconi. Box No, below.

'Ah, there you are, Sister!' Brother Cuthbert was waving her
down.

Sister Joan drew to a halt and alighted.

'I hoped I might catch you,' he said genially. 'I went down
to the presbytery to call on Father Malone and Father Stephen
– both very much better but still feeling a trifle shaky. I was just
in time to pick up two new arrivals – armed with letters from
His Lordship the Bishop and their own parish priest – also
your own Mother House in London. Two new postulants have
presented themselves.'

'Two new what?' Sister Joan said blankly.

'Postulants, Sister. New recruits for Our Blessed Lord. They
didn't realize there was no bus up to the convent and were
lugging their suitcases along with the best will in the world
when I spotted them.'

He beckoned to two figures standing at a little distance, both
wearing mackintoshes and wellingtons.

'Mother David never mentioned—' Sister Joan began.

'I suspect that recent delays in our admirable postal service
may have held up the advance information. Here they both
are if you can take them under your wing. This is Sister Joan
who is one of our little community's most treasured members.'

'Bridget Mayo, Sister. It's that lovely to get here!'

A round, freckled face, beaming goodness under a thatch of red hair, looked down at her as her hand was enthusiastically shaken.

'Bridget,' Sister Joan said.

'Anne O'Grady, Sister.'

The smaller, darker girl at her side shook hands with equal enthusiasm, her blue eyes shining.

'We were hoping to do our postulancy together,' Bridget Mayo said, threatening to pump Sister Joan's hand all over again. 'We prayed about it, didn't we, Anne? And then His Lordship approved the idea. Prayer is a wonderful thing, isn't it, Sister?'

Innocence bright as diamond flashed from them as they loaded their suituases and assorted bags into the van.

'It is indeed,' Sister Joan said.

'And the renewing of vows,' Brother Cuthbert said, smiling at her. 'All Saints' Day tomorrow, Sister! What a joy!'

'A joy and a blessing,' she agreed. 'Make sure the doors are fastened, girls. I'm not the best driver in the world. God bless, Brother Cuthbert!'

'God bless all here!' he returned. And stood, brown habit fluttering in the wind, as she drove away across the moor.